# Kussman

An aristocratic adventurer who's constantly chasing after Aria.

# Vulcan

A girl from the tiger-eared clan who runs an item shop for adventurers.

## Tama

A human man and former knight who is reincarnated as a behemoth. He's a monster of the strongest rank, but because he's still a cub, he looks like a kitten.

## Aria

A well-endowed elf girl. She found Tama while on a quest as an adventurer.

A massive body covered in jet-black fur. Two demonic horns protrude from its head, and razor-sharp fangs jut out from its jaw. Its wings, torso, and legs are all shielded by a blue-black carapace. Put simply, it's a lion with the features of a dragon—and the four-legged beast stands proudly, exuding an undeniably majestic aura.

GUOOOOOOOOOOOOOOOOOO!!

I'M A
BEHEMOTH,
an S-Ranked
MONSTER, but MISTAKEN
for a CAT, I Live as an ELF GIRL'S PET

1

Nozomi Ginyoku

Illustration by
Mitsuki Yano

YEN
ON
New York

I'm a Behemoth, an S-Ranked Monster, but Mistaken for a Cat,
I Live as an Elf Girl's Pet, Vol. 1
Nozomi Ginyoku

Translation by Caleb DeMarais
Cover art by Mitsuki Yano

This book is a work of fiction. Names, characters, places, and incidents are the product of the author's imagination or are used fictitiously. Any resemblance to actual events, locales, or persons, living or dead, is coincidental.

S RANKU MONSTAA NO BEHIIMOSU DAKEDO, NEKO TO MACHIGAWARETE ERUFU
MUSUME NO PETTO TOSHITE KURASHITEMASU volume 1
©Ginyoku Nozomi ©Yano Mitsuki ©MICRO MAGAZINE, INC.
All rights reserved.
First published in Japan in 2018 by MICRO MAGAZINE, INC.
English translation rights arranged with MICRO MAGAZINE, INC.
through Tuttle-Mori Agency, Inc., Tokyo.

English translation © 2020 by Yen Press, LLC

Yen On
150 West 30th Street, 19th Floor
New York, NY 10001

Visit us at yenpress.com
facebook.com/yenpress
twitter.com/yenpress
yenpress.tumblr.com
instagram.com/yenpress

First Yen On Edition: July 2020

Yen On is an imprint of Yen Press, LLC.
The Yen On name and logo are trademarks of Yen Press, LLC.

The publisher is not responsible for websites (or their content) that are not owned by the publisher.

Library of Congress Cataloging-in-Publication Data
Names: Ginyoku, Nozomi, author. | Yano, Mitsuki, illustrator. |
DeMarais, Caleb, translator.
Title: I'm a behemoth, an S-ranked monster, but mistaken for a cat,
I live as an elf girl's pet / Nozomi Ginyoku ; illustration by Mitsuki Yano ;
translation by Caleb DeMarais.
Other titles: S-rank monster no behemoth dakedo, neko to machigawarete elf
musume no pet toshite kurashitemasu. English | I am a behemoth, an S-ranked
monster, but mistaken for a cat, I live as an elf girl's pet
Description: First Yen On edition. | New York, NY : Yen On, 2020–
Identifiers: LCCN 2020018429 | ISBN 9781975332945 (v. 1 ; trade paperback)
Subjects: CYAC: Fantasy. | Reincarnation—Fiction. | Monsters—Fiction. |
Elves—Fiction. | Humorous stories.
Classification: LCC PZ7.1.N698 Sr 2020 | DDC [Fic]—dc23
LC record available at https://lccn.loc.gov/2020018429

ISBNs: 978-1-9753-3294-5 (paperback)
978-1-9753-3310-2 (ebook)

1 3 5 7 9 10 8 6 4 2

LSC-C

Printed in the United States of America

# CONTENTS

CHAPTER **1** I Am a Behemoth, but I Have No Name — 001

CHAPTER **2** Of Cats and Elves — 009

CHAPTER **3** Tiger-Eared Girl — 081

CHAPTER **4** From Now On as a Cat — 139

Aria's Side Story — 199

Afterword — 213

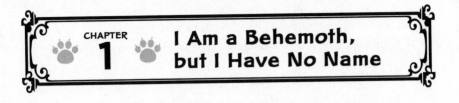

## CHAPTER 1 — I Am a Behemoth, but I Have No Name

An ashen, gloomy sky—

Barren rock and earthen walls extend in every direction while an array of monsters prowls around.

This is the labyrinth.

Its mazelike passages are twisted and convoluted enough to deserve the name—and it exhibits an eerie power that continually spawns monsters.

"Meowwwhr…?"

Today, a newborn monster issues an infant cry. But what can it be?

The creature's voice has an odd timbre.

*Where am I? Last thing I remember, I was felled by that* damn assassin's *blade…*

In its memories, the monster recalls being a knight. And in the middle of a pitched battle against demons, the enemy of humanity, it had suffered a powerful slash attack and been slain.

*But what happened after that? Did the rest of my party survive? And what of our country's fate…? Forget it. For now, I need to understand what's happening to… What the hell is this?!*

Suddenly all the monster's thoughts come to a screeching halt as it reels in shock. When it attempted to walk forward, the creature finally caught a glimpse of its feet—or rather, its paws.

Four toes covered in orange tabby fur, with sharp claws protruding from each.

Peeking with trepidation at its paw, the monster catches sight of squishy pink pads and immediately dashes off in a sprint.

It needs to find something with which to verify its body's appearance.

The search takes only a moment.

A pool of water quickly comes into view, causing the monster to shriek in shock—"Meowwwwhr...?!"

It sees its reflection staring back with wide eyes—the reflection of a kitten.

*Status!* the monster silently screams in its mind. In response, a number of words appear in its field of vision.

"Status" is a self-analytical magic spell. Previously, as a knight, the monster could use the spell to ascertain its current condition. Apparently, the spell still works because the following appears:

---

**Name: None**
**Type: Behemoth (cub)**
**Innate Skills: None**

---

*A be...behemoth?!*

The monster...no, the behemoth lets loose a shocked roar. Behemoths are S-ranked monsters.

Aside from a few exceptions, monsters are ranked according to how dangerous they're considered, going from E to S. A general breakdown is as follows:

E rank = Monsters that the average person could defeat as long as they are properly equipped.

D rank = Monsters that will be difficult to defeat for anyone lacking combat experience.

C rank = Monsters that usually require at least several well-equipped warriors to defeat. Only accomplished veterans can challenge these monsters and hope to come out on top.

B rank = Monsters that could easily wipe out a small village. Powerful skills are generally required to deal with them.

A rank = Monsters that could easily raze an entire urban area. Although there are exceptions, defeating them usually calls for several warriors with high-level tactics and powerful skills.

S rank = Monsters with enough power to possibly ruin entire nations. Confronting them usually requires states to assemble all available forces. Only a hero or someone comparable could even think of facing them alone.

In other words, a behemoth is classified as one of the highest-ranked monsters. Behemoths inspire such dread that they're sometimes thought of as natural disasters.

*I should be dead, but now I'm a monster... This must be the reincarnation that I've heard so much about...*

In this world, living things can be reborn after death.

The behemoth begins to grasp that this is exactly what has happened. Myriad thoughts flood its mind. Receiving the chance at a second life is surely something to be thankful for. Still, to think that reincarnation would mean coming back in the form of a monster, the sworn enemy of humanity...unbelievable.

Unfortunately, the behemoth doesn't have any time to waste feeling distraught.

Why?

"Ghghwa!"

"Gya-gwa-gwa-hhha!"

Those voices belong to the behemoth's enemies.

Two goblins appear, both trailing strings of drool that hang from their mouths. They have green skin and childlike bodies—E-ranked monsters.

The behemoth observes them.

*There's no doubt these two want to eat me.*

And then—

This is a serious predicament. Top-class monster or not, the behemoth is currently a cub with meager physical strength and no knowledge of how to use its powerful innate skills.

At this rate, the poor beast will be ripped to shreds and eaten as raw meat.

…If it was a normal behemoth, that is.

"Meowww!" *Don't underestimate me, goblins!*

The behemoth cries out in an adorable voice and burrows its gaze into the goblins with cute eyes. Seeing this, both goblins emit a grating cry, "Gya-gwa-gwa-ha!" as if they can't believe their own eyes.

The goblins rush toward the behemoth, both brandishing daggers.

"G-gwaaa!"

One of the goblins swings its blade. An ordinary behemoth cub would have been felled with that one blow, its life forfeit. However, residing inside the body of this behemoth is the spirit of a battle-worn knight. This cub will not be easy prey.

The behemoth predicts the incoming dagger's path in an instant and sidesteps the attack with ease. After completing that maneuver, it rushes toward the goblin who struck nothing but air. Aiming for its knees, the behemoth rams its head into the goblin with all its might.

"Gu-gwaaa?!!"

The goblin, startled by the counterattack, cries out at the sharp pain running up its thigh before crumpling to the ground.

*Ngh...that was rather painful. I should avoid using too many charge attacks.*

The impact of the headbutt has also left the behemoth in pain, but that doesn't stop it.

"G-gwaaaa!!"

Seeing its companion lying on the ground and grasping an injured shin, the second goblin roars in anger. Holding its dagger at an angle—neither straight-up nor level—the monster charges the behemoth, intent on slicing it to shreds.

"Meow!" *This is my chance!*

Tracking the dagger's tip, the behemoth flips into the air. Arcing gracefully, it flies toward the goblin, whose blade cuts harmlessly through the space directly below.

And then—

*Snikt!*

The razor-sharp claws extending from the behemoth's teeny front legs sink into the goblin's eyes, eliciting a scream that rattles the labyrinth. The reaction is only natural, given the blinding pain and loss of sight that's thrown the monster into utter confusion.

"Meow." *Let's see now—let me test one of my innate skills, shall I?*

As the goblins writhe in agony, the behemoth decides to try using one of its skills. It chooses "Elemental Howl." What sort of skill might it be?

Concentrating on the skill's name and preparing to let loose a howl, the behemoth notices a few words appear in its field of vision.

**Elemental Howl:  (1) Flame Howl (2) Aqua Howl
(3) Aether Howl (4) Rock Howl**

*     *     *

*Hmm. Judging by these names, it seems I can activate various elemental skills. Looks like I can choose from fire, water, wind, or stone. Let's use Flame Howl here. I haven't the slightest clue as to how effective it might be, but I suspect it's the strongest.*

"Meowwww!" *Flame Howl!*

The resulting sound is honestly too precious to be called a howl.

*Boom—!!*

However, a thunderous peal springs from the behemoth, and a scorching flame erupts alongside its howl. The firestorm engulfs both goblins for a few moments, leaving nothing behind but ash and dust.

"Meowrrr." *Is it really possible to be this strong as a mere cub?!*

The behemoth is shocked at the completely unexpected level of power. It certainly appears to be a bona fide S-ranked monster.

*I lack a purpose, a goal. For now, I will simply do my best to survive. There must be a reason I was reborn with this body.*

The behemoth initially felt dismal after discovering it had been reborn as a monster, but for the moment, it's resolved to focus on staying alive.

The behemoth raises its voice in a cry.

"Meyooow!!"

The behemoth's howl—

This roar is the beginning of the tale of the unrivaled Strongest Cat that will be passed on to future generations.

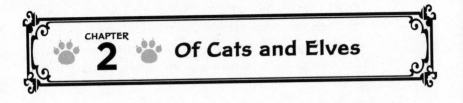

"Meow! ♪ Meow! ♪ Meow... ♪"

Walking through the labyrinth, the behemoth is in high spirits despite having quite a few reasons for distress and worry.

Discovering his natural strength is certainly a factor, but there are also others.

*What a nimble and comfortable body!*

The behemoth's head moves much more nimbly than when he was a human—no matter how much he moves his head, there's no sense of fatigue.

What's more, even though other monsters attacked after the earlier run-in with goblins, the behemoth's innate skill Elemental Howl allowed him to use Flame Howl, defeating every challenger in a single blast.

*And this is definitely an S-ranked monster's body! Exactly how much mana is hiding inside this small frame...?*

*Mana*—the life energy that resides within all living beings in this world.

When using skills or magic, every creature—whether human, demon, or monster—must consume this mana. The amount of mana that must be spent increases according to the power or effect of the skills or magic used.

The behemoth has already activated Flame Howl several times, but there is still no sign of the mana inside his body being depleted at all—even after repeatedly invoking that powerful flame.

One of the reasons the behemoth is so incredibly fearsome lies in this massive reserve of mana.

"Meowr?" *Hmm, what's that?*

The behemoth stops in his tracks upon noticing a new monster peeking out from the shadow of a rock outcropping. It's a transparent, round blob known as a slime.

This is an E-ranked monster, just like the goblins.

*Another monster, eh? I've seen so many—it must be because this is a labyrinth.*

Rocky surfaces spread in every direction, riddled with mazelike paths. Given the high frequency of encountering monsters here, the behemoth concludes that this must indeed be a labyrinth.

By now, the behemoth has decided on his goal: to get the hell out of here.

The behemoth has been blessed with another (cat) life. There's no way he plans to spend it in a place as bleak as this.

Once his mind is made up, the rest comes quickly—the behemoth settles on two things he must do.

First—continue exploring.

Leaving the labyrinth is easier said than done. As mentioned before, the place is a gargantuan maze. Escaping means finding one of the exits, of which there should be several. Until then, even a behemoth needs a safe place to sleep.

To that end, the behemoth needs to familiarize himself with the surrounding paths.

Second—training.

The behemoth is a powerful monster, but he's still a cub.

Facing low-level monsters like the goblins he defeated are one thing, but against a high-level monster, the behemoth cub might lose before getting a chance to utilize any powerful skills.

There's also a high possibility of eventually coming across humans outside the labyrinth. Some humans called adventurers make a living off slaying monsters and selling the harvested materials.

Aside from certain special exceptions, adventurers are classified from rank E to S just like monsters. If the behemoth runs into a high-level adventurer, he'll probably get hunted down.

That's why the behemoth must hone his battle skills on low-level monsters and get used to his new body, while also training up and becoming stronger.

*However, I was also once human. I don't want to fight any if I can help it.*

If worse comes to worst, the behemoth might one day be forced to kill what he still considers to be a fellow human...

Due to a strong sense of justice in his previous life, the behemoth meekly mewls "Meow..." at the mere thought.

But enough of that. The behemoth must turn his attention to his current enemy, which is only a few feet away.

*This time it's a slime, hmm? If I recall correctly, I'll need to destroy the core at the center of its body. Maybe I should scorch it using Flame Howl... No, wait... Since this is a new enemy, I should test out a different skill.*

The slime moves slowly and has very low attack power—far weaker than those two goblins. It's the perfect enemy to practice skills on.

"Meowhr!"

The behemoth shouts, drawing the attention of the slime that responds with "Pikii!" while closing in at an excruciatingly slow crawl (not that it has any legs).

*Okay, here it comes!*

The behemoth lets out another cry, essentially revealing to the slime his exact location, but this is all part of a strategy to make aiming his skill easier.

The slime takes the bait. This blob looks perfectly harmless, but it's still a frightening monster. Now aware of the nearby behemoth's soft flesh, it's focused on devouring its prey.

"Meow!" *Rock Howl!*

Once the slime comes quite close, the behemoth activates another of his Elemental Howls, Rock Howl. As the behemoth lets out a cute growl, a load of rocks hurtles toward the slime.

*"Pikii?!"*

The slime cries out and freezes in place. One of the flying missiles blows right through its transparent body and pierces the core—its heart.

*Hmm. It's no Flame Howl, but this skill is strong, too—it took only a single shot to penetrate a slime's body, which has shock-absorption properties. A behemoth's innate skills are something else!*

The behemoth nods in great satisfaction at the superb results.

*Gurgle—*

A dainty noise emits from the behemoth's stomach.

*Come to think of it, I haven't eaten a single thing since I was reincarnated. Thankfully, all monsters are omnivores from what I recall. I guess I'll tear into this one right here.*

Eating monsters...and a slime, at that. Making a meal of such a strange creature would turn anyone's stomach. At the same time, the behemoth must find food soon and doesn't know when the next chance will present itself.

The behemoth cautiously sniffs the dead slime. There's a curious odor, but it seems safe, at least.

After becoming a monster, the behemoth found his olfactory senses had become much sharper, and the same could be said of his instinctive ability to predict danger.

*Chommmp!*

Some say men should have strong stomachs, but they probably didn't mean it quite so literally. The behemoth grits his teeth and rips into the slime.

*This is…surprisingly sweet?!*

The behemoth's golden eyes go wide as saucers.

Turns out, this is what slimes taste like. The behemoth assumed it would be bitter or nasty, making this discovery a pleasant surprise.

Moreover, the slime has a nice texture, landing somewhere between fruit jelly and a gummy bear.

*This is delicious!*

The behemoth tears into the slime again, stuffing his tiny mouth, munching away, and making little chewing noises—truly an adorable sight.

From this scene alone, no one would imagine that this creature is one of the most feared monsters, a behemoth.

"Meowr?" *Hmm? What is this?*

Right as he goes in for another bite, the behemoth notices an abnormality.

The words *Skill Absorb* have appeared in his field of vision.

*Did I just activate a skill? But all I'm doing is eating a slime. Nothing seems to have happened… What's this all about?*

There's no trace of any skills being activated, and nothing about the behemoth himself has changed.

After a brief moment of thought, the behemoth arrives at a possibility.

*Hmm... Oh! Maybe it's a status-based skill?!*

A status-based skill is a general term for abilities that can increase attack power or defensive ability—among other changes in status, as the name implies.

"Meow!" *Status!*

To confirm what's happening, the behemoth casts Status, the self-analysis spell. The following appears:

---

**Name: None**
**Type: Behemoth (cub)**
**Innate Skills: Elemental Howl, Skill Absorb**
**Absorbed Skills: Storage**

---

*...There's no entry for status changes. I guess it wasn't a status-based skill?*

Normally, a line for status changes should appear after any status variation occurs, but it hasn't shown up this time.

In other words, the behemoth's innate skill Skill Absorb doesn't cause any change in status.

*In that case, just what does this skill do? If it's not a status-based skill, then... Wait a second—what in the world?!*

Just as the behemoth is about to close the status display, he notices something.

*There's more now... My skills have increased!!*

Upon being reincarnated, the behemoth noticed he only had innate skills. But what about now? In the entry after innate skills—the line for absorbed skills—it now reads *Storage*, doesn't it?!

*That must be it!*

Just then, the behemoth realizes something unique to the

arcane nature of the behemoth species. Behemoths are fearsome monsters, but more than that, they are deeply mysterious.

The mystery lies in the fact that each individual behemoth can activate wildly varying sets of skills. In other words, every encounter with a new behemoth is different because it's impossible to know what type of skills they might use.

All this means that there's no established way of dealing with behemoths or strategies for fighting them. This is the principal reason they are considered S-ranked monsters.

Naturally, this behemoth has just solved that mystery. The path to increasing his power has become clear. After eating an enemy, using his innate skill—Skill Absorb...

*Okay, let's try it out!*

The behemoth stares at the slime he was eating and activates his new skill, Storage.

And then—

The slime's corpse completely disappears. The behemoth, now realizing what Storage actually means, activates the skill again.

The results are as expected. The slime's corpse appears once again.

Slimes have the ability to draw foreign matter inside their bodies and store it for later. The behemoth also has that power now after absorbing that very same skill.

*Incredible! This means that eating monsters will allow me to absorb and use any skill in the world!*

As the immense potential for growth dawns on the behemoth, he lets loose a roar of joy. "Meeeooowowrrrrrrh!"

*Okay, let's keep the rest of this slime for an afternoon snack.*

Having confirmed the effects of his new skill, the behemoth stashes the slime away for later and starts licking his front legs... and, without realizing it, keeps rubbing his face repeatedly with his paws.

Put simply, he's acting on the instinctive need that all felines share to groom after a meal.

Despite being a human in his previous life, the behemoth doesn't find it at all strange to clean his face thanks to these new instincts.

"Meowwwwnnn…!"

After finishing taking care of his face, the behemoth stretches out just like a cat, looking perfectly content. Maybe it's to be expected immediately following a meal, but…the behemoth seems really sleepy.

*Hmph. I feel extraordinarily tired. Come to think of it, I've essentially just been born. Running around this much and using so many skills—it's no wonder I'm tired. Right, I need to find a place to rest for the night as soon as possible. Hopefully, I'll happen upon some cozy, dark corner…*

The behemoth stumbles forward in search of a place to rest, rubbing his sleepy eyes.

*Living in the body of a monster for a little while makes me realize…daily life for humans is truly blessed.*

The behemoth was a no-nonsense knight in his past life but also had a fair share of indulgences. Once work was over, all the knights would often go drinking together, and days off meant a chance to enjoy lazing about idly. Nights were occupied by tucking in to somewhat pricey but wholly delicious dinners, regaining lost energy to be ready for the next day.

In stark contrast, the knight now finds himself reborn as a monster.

Simply surviving demands every iota of time and effort. Luxuries and pastimes are a far-off dream.

*Well, I suppose things could be worse…*

There's no doubt that being reborn as an S-ranked monster like a behemoth is a stroke of good fortune, and to be blessed with his past life's memories on top of that is nothing to sneeze at, either.

Without the combat experience from that previous life—

Without the knowledge of all the skills honed by knighthood—

There's a decent chance the behemoth would have been slaughtered by that first goblin encounter.

*Oh, I see. Maybe that's why there are so few behemoths out there.*

The behemoth realizes again that, as a cub, there's not much difference between him and a newborn kitten. Aside from his powerful innate skills, the behemoth's physical prowess pales in comparison to other monsters'.

In short, most behemoths probably lose their lives before ever reaching adulthood. This must be why the former knight never heard much about behemoth cubs in his past life, and he only realized his new identity after seeing it spelled out on the status display.

*Oh, this looks like a decent spot.*

After walking for some time, the behemoth spots a rocky crag in his peripheral field of vision. There's a hollow divot in the ground leading up to it, and the depression looks relatively deep, which should hide him from enemies. For a behemoth, this is the perfect resting place.

Now that he can finally sleep, the behemoth mews with glee.

"Meow! ♪ Meow! ♪"

Unfortunately, at that exact moment—

—an ice-cold, indescribable sense of dread runs up his back. He has a terrible premonition and leaps away from the rocky crag with a small yelp.

Moments later, a large black figure drops from the sky and lands with a *thud* in front of him.

*Whoa?! A poison serpent...!!*

The behemoth's eyes grow wide.

The creature bearing down on him is a poison serpent—approximately fifteen feet in length, with deadly venomous fangs. It's a C-ranked monster.

Glaring at the behemoth, the poison serpent emits a threatening snarl.

"Hisssss."

The serpent had been hanging on the ceiling, lying in wait for a chance to devour the behemoth.

*A C-ranked monster... This shouldn't be impossible. Plus, it's a good opportunity to test out my remaining innate skills!*

Making up his mind to accept the serpent's challenge, the behemoth steps forward to begin the assault.

"Meow!" *Aqua Howl!*

A compressed blast of water rushes from the behemoth's mouth as his roar rings out.

Perhaps sensing danger in the behemoth's movements, the serpent coils up to avoid the attack. That was the right choice—Aqua Howl completely misses its mark and rockets into a distant wall. It erupts in a splash and leaves a notch in the rocky surface.

The intense impact of Aqua Howl brings to mind the image of a geyser.

*Damn, it evaded my attack. Well, try this one on for size!*

The behemoth was once a knight who was a veteran of countless battles. He's not the type to falter just because an opponent saw through one of his moves.

He roars again, "Meow!"—but nothing happens. At least, the poison serpent doesn't think so. But it is wrong.

The serpent draws itself up high and charges toward the behemoth. That's when it happens— Right when the monster's mouth is gaping wide, ready to attack, its massive body is sent flying.

This is due to the behemoth activating Aether Howl. The attack causes the surrounding air to converge on a single target, kind of like an invisible missile made of wind.

The sheer force blasts the poison serpent into the craggy rock wall behind it. Bashing its head into the hard surface, the monster loses consciousness immediately, foaming at the mouth.

"Meow…" *Serves you right for spoiling my nap…*

The behemoth approaches the serpent, still stunned from the blow.

Staring down with his narrow feline pupils…

*Fwap!!*

…the behemoth activates Aqua Howl and blasts a fierce jet of water directly into the poison serpent's face.

*Okay, before I sleep, let's have a bite of this thing. Who knows, I might obtain a new skill.*

The behemoth rips into the serpent's belly with his jaws.

Blech. *Bitter. And the texture resembles tough chicken skin.*

The serpent turns out to be somewhat unpalatable. The behemoth chews what's left in his mouth, swallowing loudly. Then, to finish it off, he uses Flame Howl to burn the corpse to ash.

*At any rate, better check my status. Let's see… Oh! I've gained another one!*

---

**Name: None**
**Type: Behemoth (cub)**
**Innate Skills: Elemental Howl, Skill Absorb**
**Absorbed Skills: Storage, Poison Fang**

---

*Poison Fang… Judging from the name, it sounds like I'll be able to inject my own fangs with a venom of some sort. But I'm still a cub* and rather weak. *The reach of this skill is too short. I don't think I'll have a chance to use it yet.*

The behemoth is slightly disappointed.

*Oh well. I've found a place to sleep, so I should be satisfied.*

It's important to remain positive. That goes for both humans and monsters. The behemoth tells himself this and burrows into the hollow cavity by the rocky crag, starting to snore almost immediately.

The monster battles will only continue from here. Better to rest up now.

*Okay, which path should I take?*

After the behemoth wakes from his slumber, he finds a forked road before him. This is a crucial decision—one could lead to an escape from the labyrinth, while the other could take him deeper into the maze.

*Still, there isn't anything here I can base my decision on. I'll have to go with my gut.*

The behemoth ultimately chooses to head to the right. After following the path for a while, he notices his surroundings changing slightly.

The rocky walls become striated with an array of colors, laced with geometric shapes and the ancient writing of this world. Depictions of various monsters and humans battling them also coat the walls.

*Hmm... Could this be where the labyrinth dwellers once lived?*

Labyrinth dwellers were an ancient people who settled in the labyrinth. The specific reasons or goals behind their migration have gone undiscovered. There are several standing theories—they might have possessed a culture that aspired to live alongside monsters, or perhaps they wanted to understand the ecosystems that monsters lived within so they could study and harness them for a military advantage.

*Wait, that's…!!*

The behemoth's eyes grow wide. A hulking presence has just entered his field of vision, sporting steely skin and massive legs. Differing from regular monsters, this creature doesn't act of its own volition but instead exists as a guardian, unfailingly protecting a specific area.

The monster, known as a golem, roars thunderously.

*"Grooooaaaarrrrr!!"*

Two deep indentations are where most would expect the golem's eyes to be in its steel face, and the red light emanating from them bores into the behemoth. It would seem the behemoth has already set foot into forbidden territory.

The golem's legs thunder against the ground as it lumbers toward the behemoth. It's surprisingly fast despite its dull, heavy presence.

*Crap—retreat!*

The behemoth changes direction immediately and runs at full speed.

There is a way to take the golem down. A magic script is engraved into the golem's head, and erasing even a single letter of it will terminate the golem's functions.

But the behemoth is extremely tiny. Even with Elemental Howl, there's no chance he'll have the range to reach the massive monster's only weak point, the magic script.

Running at full speed should be more effective—the behemoth can probably shake the golem.

Without his human knowledge of monsters, he might have recklessly tried attacking the golem and wound up squashed flat.

*It's no use—I'll have to double back and take the left-hand path.*

Having returned to the fork in the road, the behemoth turns onto the opposite path. This time, the environment around him doesn't change, with rocky outcroppings appearing in every direction. But there is one difference—the width of the path. The farther along he gets, the wider the path becomes.

Before long, the behemoth can see a large cavern. It's not exactly massive…but it has a relatively high ceiling, meaning that significantly large monsters wouldn't have a problem maneuvering in the chamber.

And then—a piercing, shrill cry erupts.

"Gggygyaaaaah!!"

*It's a wyvern!*

The monster appears diagonally across from the behemoth, who clicks his tongue in a muted meow.

The wyvern has gray scales reminiscent of a reptile and massive wings, as well as fierce claws extending from its hind legs. It's a low-level winged dragon.

But low-level or not, a dragon is a dragon. It's a B rank and has the power to ravage a small village.

Faced with such a monster, the behemoth decides to retreat again…or most would assume—

His fur bristling, the behemoth directs his golden eyes at the wyvern with a hateful glare. He's planning to fight it head-on. He only just fled from a golem because his skills didn't have the proper range. How does he expect to face a wyvern, a far deadlier enemy?

"Gyaohhh!!"

The wyvern's face seems to say *Fool!* as it screeches and hurtles down through the air to attack the behemoth, who reverses and manages to avoid its grasp. The behemoth's movements have gotten snappier. He's gotten used to his new body after all the battles he's fought thus far.

*You're dead wrong. Why don't you fly down even farther?*

The behemoth thinks this to himself and charges forward. He dashes to the left and right, then runs in a circle, intermittently crying "Meowrrr!!" to taunt the wyvern.

"Groawww!!"

The wyvern is furious at being mocked by a monster so much weaker than itself. With an angry screech, it flies up close to the ceiling and extends its claws fully while tucking in its wings before swooping down at the behemoth with terrifying speed.

On such short legs, there's no way the behemoth can evade. Or can he? The behemoth doesn't seem panicked whatsoever. Instead, he's calmly pointing his mouth up at a slight angle.

"Meow!" *This is it!*

Just as he yips, the behemoth forces all the air he's stored in his lungs out in one massive blast.

Then—

A gale of air fills the chamber with a *fwoom!!* "Gyaaaaarh!" The wyvern screams in shock as it gets blown in every direction.

Finally, it plummets to the earth. Not understanding what's just happened, the wyvern falls back onto basic survival instinct, preparing to launch itself up again.

But there's a problem with that. Having been blasted across the room, the wyvern's inner ear has been thrown out of whack. It can't even stand without stumbling.

Just as the wyvern dived down toward him, the behemoth unleashed Aether Howl. He had aimed for the wyvern's *left wing*, landing a direct hit that sent the wyvern sprawling.

Why didn't he use a different Elemental Howl to bring it down? There's a good reason—the behemoth realized that different skills take a different amount of time to activate. From fastest to slowest, they rank: (1) Aether Howl, (2) Aqua Howl, (3) Rock Howl, and (4) Flame Howl.

It appears the lung capacity needed for each spell varies according to their strength—practically speaking, that's the amount of time needed to activate them.

Aether Howl is the fastest of the bunch. The behemoth can use it after holding his breath for just a brief moment. In order to retaliate against the wyvern's unique attack-and-retreat pattern that takes advantage of its flying ability, Aether Howl was the only choice.

A full-grown behemoth would have many more options to choose from...but let's forget about that for now. The behemoth focuses on the wyvern, which is struggling to even stand steadily, centering his target in his vision while inhaling deeply.

Then—

"Meow!" *Rock Howl!*

He unleashes a massive earth Elemental Howl. A cascade of large rocks shoots from the behemoth's mouth, mercilessly pelting the wyvern—tearing into its belly, face, and wings, forcing the very breath from its body...

*Nice. Time to take a bite.*

The wyvern's corpse lies still like an empty beehive, allowing the behemoth to rip into its flesh as drool dribbles from his jaws.

Among humans, the wyvern's flesh is bought and sold as the highest-quality meat available. It has a rich flavor paired with incredible texture, making for a truly delicious delicacy. Although the behemoth is devouring it raw, he's very happy to be eating something humans also enjoy.

*Hmm? What's this?*

After savoring his fill of the wyvern, the behemoth's eyes

grow wide at the status display that has appeared in his field of vision.

The behemoth's abilities have changed as follows:

---

**Name: None**
**Type: Behemoth (cub)**
**Innate Skills: Elemental Howl, Skill Absorb,**
   **Elemental Tail Blade**
**Absorbed Skills: Storage, Poison Fang, Flight**

---

The entry Elemental Tail Blade has been added to innate skills, and Flight has been added to absorbed skills.

*Flight is simple to explain—the ability to fly, gained through Skill Absorb by eating the wyvern's flesh. But Elemental Tail Blade... What could this be?*

The skills absorbed through consuming a defeated monster's flesh have all fallen into the absorbed skills category so far. But this time, a skill was added to the innate skills list.

The behemoth's tail curls into a puzzled question mark. He has good reason to be perplexed—monsters and humans are completely different biologically.

What does this all mean? We should begin by discussing the differences between humans and monsters.

Human skills can be divided into two broad categories.

The first includes hereditary or congenital skills. The second includes skills that can be learned through magic items called scrolls and are acquired a posteriori. Exceptions that fall outside this framework do exist...but they're extremely rare.

As far as monsters go...their skills can also be divided into two categories.

The first is the same as humans—skills they are born with. The second consists of *new* skills that require experiences on the battlefield to acquire.

Far different from humans, monsters constantly come face-to-face with death. They are always increasing their abilities and can learn new skills without the support of items.

There is a limit and a set of rules governing what skills monsters can learn. Exceptions to this are few in number… Perhaps the only loophole is the innate skill Skill Absorb, which behemoths possess.

*No matter. I'll put the skills that are immediately effective to use. Let's try out this new one…*

"Meow!" *Flight!*

The behemoth mews adorably and activates the skill. In an instant, jet-black wings reminiscent of reptile skin sprout from his orange tabby feline back.

*Wow, I already know how to move these wings—and how to fly!*

The second the wings materialized, the behemoth understood through feral instinct how to use them.

He whips the wings out in a flash, fully extending them. Bringing his center of gravity forward, he launches himself from the stony ground with a sharp kick.

Success—

A sensation of floating comes over him, accompanied by a rush of speed running through his entire body. The behemoth has taken to the sky beautifully.

*This feels amazing…! And although it's imperceptible, I can feel mana coursing around my body.*

As the behemoth begins turning in the sky, he realizes what this probably means. The flow of magical energy around him—it's wind mana that he's generating himself!

His newly acquired skill Flight doesn't simply grant the ability to grow wings and fly.

The behemoth is still a cub. When he grows into an adult, he'll be able to grow wings incomparably tougher and larger, but his current body isn't actually built to fly.

The Flight skill allows him to sustain flight despite this by creating a thin layer of mana to protect him from low air temperature and wind resistance.

*Truly a shame. If only Elemental Howl had better range, I would be able to rain pure destruction on my enemies from far above...*

The behemoth can't stop thinking about it. If his innate skill Elemental Howl could hit farther away, he'd be able to attack from the skies without even getting close to his enemies.

Unfortunately, the behemoth's Elemental Howl only has middling reach. Attacking from a distance while flying simply isn't practical.

*I can't change something that's impossible. I'll settle on testing my other new skill for now.*

It's important for humans and monsters alike to know when to give up. The behemoth recognizes this as he floats gently down to the ground. He ceases using his Flight skill simply by thinking as much, and the jet-black wings disappear in an instant.

*Okay, let's see what this Elemental Tail Blade is all about. I'm assuming it's quite similar to Elemental Howl?*

As the behemoth activates Elemental Tail Blade, it unfolds exactly as he expected.

**Elemental Tail Blade:  Flame Edge, Aqua Edge, Aether Edge, Rock Edge**

A secondary status display appears. From their names, it's clear that four different elemental skills can be cast, just like Elemental Howl.

*I'll start here, with the one I know I'll love.*

"Meow!" *Flame Edge!*

The behemoth cries out energetically, and seconds later, his tail is on fire—no, embers have surrounded his tail. In the next instant, the blaze converges into a single blade of surging red flame.

*This is...just like a magic sword! It must be over six feet long...*

A magic sword is exactly what it sounds like—a weapon formed by magic power, able to take on a wide assortment of different elements, just like the behemoth's tail at present.

Strictly speaking, a magic sword is purely made of magic. In contrast, the behemoth's Elemental Tail Blade doesn't rely on any magical energy. It's simply a skill, so while it is similar to a magic sword, it's also different.

The behemoth swipes his tail through the air—how does it feel? The surging flame sword slices at blinding speed, accompanied by an audible rush. The behemoth's eyes go wide. He didn't even concentrate on speed when swinging his tail, but the result was lightning fast...

In his previous life, the behemoth's swordsmanship was among the best of his entire unit. Yet the move he just pulled off with his tail could be considered on the same level... It might have been better, even.

And it should be. As a knight, he wielded the sword with his hands. Now, with Elemental Tail Blade, it's no exaggeration to say the sword is just another part of his body.

Moreover, it's located in his most flexible appendage—his tail can bend in every direction possible. Calling it easy to maneuver is an understatement.

*And that's not all. This skill... It doesn't even require a charge-up period the way Elemental Howl does. The speed I can activate this with is on a completely different level. Plus, it seems the skill can be used indefinitely, until dispelled by the user... Heh-heh-heh, as someone who previously lived by the sword, this is the best skill I could ask for!!*

The behemoth once entrusted his life to the sword—now that it's a part of his monster body, he'll be able to reach new dimensions of mastery. The behemoth can feel his blood surge throughout his body, his knightly spirit emboldened.

*Okay, I definitely have the hang of it now. Next, I simply must cut something down.*

After practicing Flame Edge for a moment, the behemoth decides to take his testing to the next level.

The behemoth saunters over toward a nearby wall.

*Okay, here goes!*

The behemoth raises his Flame Edge tail in a high arc and cleaves into the rock wall. As a result, the wall hisses as it nearly vaporizes on contact. The sensation... It almost feels like slicing through butter.

*What incredible heat! This is not a normal magic sword. I must exercise caution when using it, or else...*

This has exceeded all expectations. The behemoth is slack-jawed from the sheer heat and seeing how keen the edge of his summoned blade is.

Time for the next one. The behemoth dispels the Flame Edge and tests out the next Elemental Tail Blade.

"Meow!" *Aqua Edge!*

Just like with Flame Edge, the moment the skill is activated, water converges around the behemoth's tail, forming a crystal-clear sword made of water with a similar reach—about six feet.

To compare its sharpness to Flame Edge, the behemoth slashes into the rock wall again with Aqua Edge. This skill doesn't emit the same powerful rush...but it certainly leaves a significant gouge in the wall.

*Hmm. This doesn't have the same level of power as Flame Edge, but it seems to be both quicker to activate and to slash. Just like with Elemental Howl, the ease with which I can use these skills changes according to their overall power. That means in terms of speed...*

The behemoth knows what to expect as he activates the next Elemental Tail Sword—Aether Edge.

And his assumptions were correct—no, they were exceeded. The moment he consciously decided to activate the skill, it was already complete.

His tail does not change color, but the behemoth understands that it has become a sword.

*So light. Just like I inferred from the name, this is really a blade made of air. It almost seems to have no mass or heft to it at all.*

The behemoth swings the Aether Edge. It's airy beyond imagination. As it should be—Aether Edge creates atmospheric current when slashed, allowing it to increase in speed as it flows through the air.

The Aether Edge slices through the air in an instant and takes a chunk out of the rock wall, just like Aqua Edge. However, it only does surface damage. As expected, similar to the Elemental Howl Aether Howl, the wind elemental skills are the weakest.

*Still, this is incredible. It might be weaker, but it's faster than any regular sword I've ever seen. Not to mention, the Aether Edge is a sword composed of the atmosphere... In other words, it's invisible. If my opponent doesn't have exceptional mana-sensing capabilities, they won't even know that I've activated it.*

Regular monsters tend to focus on outward strength and will likely fail to recognize the power of the Aether Edge. On the other hand, the behemoth was a human in his past life—and an accomplished swordsman at that.

There's no way the true potential of such a powerful weapon would escape his notice.

Lastly, the behemoth tests the earth elemental skill, Rock Edge. If basing it off the characteristics of Elemental Howl, its activation speed should be third—should be, that is…

*Huh? This skill is slow. And what the hell is this…?!*

Seeing the form of Rock Edge being activated, the behemoth's eyes grow wide. It's far longer than the other Elemental Tail Blade skills—almost ten feet long. It's also vastly wider than expected and made from highly polished stone.

Compared to the Elemental Tail Blade skills he's seen so far, this one is definitely the closest to an actual sword. That said, it's a bit unwieldy and would probably be categorized as a greatsword.

*No matter, let's put it to the test. Oof…it's heavy as hell.*

As the behemoth raises the Rock Edge into the air, his balance falters slightly, but he quickly regains his footing.

Before being reincarnated, he had accumulated plenty of experience with greatswords. Drawing on this wealth of knowledge, he is able to adjust his center of gravity from what's best suited for wielding a longsword to something better suited for hefting a greatsword.

The Rock Edge blade slams down through the air. The behemoth notices considerable air resistance as he smashes it directly into the wall. He should have known—the sound that reverberates through the labyrinth is closer to a bludgeoning attack than a slash.

A massive crack runs down the wall that suffered the earth elemental blade strike, and it crumbles to the ground in several places.

*Hmm, I see. Much harder to wield than the others, but it's an epic blade. I should be able to smash through even the hardest monster armor with this skill. Even if the armor holds, the attack will still deal heavy damage. Elemental Tail Blade…what an amazing skill I've been blessed with.*

The behemoth is once again in awe of another high-level innate skill he's acquired. In that moment, he realizes something.

He's amassed a number of new skills… If he unleashes them, he should be able to vanquish even *that thing*…

*Ngh…*

The behemoth has turned around on his path, with a certain objective in mind, when three enemies appear before him— minotaurs.

The one at their fore wields a massive battle-ax and swings down, dead set on the behemoth.

*You handle the ax rather well. But how naive!*

The behemoth steps back from the minotaur's swing and evades. The ax misses its target and slams into the ground, plumes of dust kicking up a moment later.

But then something curious happens.

"Mwooohhh?!"

One minotaur in the rear is shocked.

The surprise is only natural—the monster's comrade, emerging from the cloud of dust…no longer has a head.

*I'm not finished yet!*

The behemoth rushes out from just in front of the now-headless minotaur's feet. The dust storm and the reason the minotaur's head separated from its torso are both the result of the behemoth activating Aether Edge.

The wind elemental blade's formation blasted a swath of dust into the air and tore directly through the leading minotaur's neck.

"Mwooohhh!!"

They don't yet fully understand why, but their instincts tell the minotaurs that the behemoth is incredibly dangerous. They distance themselves from him.

In that moment, one of them raises its ax. Gauging the monster's movement, the behemoth infers what it's about to do.

"Mwoo…" *Fireball!*

*Magic, I knew it!!*

The behemoth is aware that some minotaurs can use magic, and while distancing himself from the minotaur with its weapon raised high, he'd already deduced it was going to cast a spell.

A molten red fireball flies at the behemoth. Of course, there's no way he would go down without a fight.

By the time he realized his enemy was launching an attack, the behemoth had already begun charging up another.

"Meow!" *Aether Howl!*

He releases the air stored in his lungs in an instant to activate Aether Howl, blasting the fireball intended for him back at his enemy with tremendous force. The fireball shoots back at the same speed—no, even faster than before.

There's nothing the minotaur can do to deal with this sudden turn of events—the very fireball it had cast hits the minotaur squarely in the face. Clawing at it, the monster attempts to scream but can't even muster a voice.

"…………!!!!!"

The minotaur flails around frantically from the excruciating pain.

A sharp slash rings out. "*Whoosh!*"

The sound has come from close to the chest of the flailing minotaur. A profuse amount of blood is gushing from it. It goes without saying that the behemoth's Aether Blade is the cause.

*Next!*

The behemoth pulls his invisible blade from the minotaur's chest and stares down its final remaining comrade.

In response, the last minotaur turns sharply on its heels and sprints in the direction from whence it came. It seems the monster finally understands after watching two comrades get obliterated—the minotaurs were the ones being hunted.

"Mweor!" *As if you're getting away!*

Naturally, the minotaurs had intended the behemoth's life. There's absolutely no chance he'd simply let one escape now.

The minotaur sprints on its powerful legs. To catch up with it, the behemoth activates his newly acquired skill Flight.

The minotaur is running while avoiding the perilous footfalls of the labyrinth, while the behemoth is soaring through the air, free of obstruction. He catches up immediately.

"Mwooohhh!" *Icicle Lance!!*

The minotaur is cornered. In desperation, it casts a mid-level water elemental spell, Icicle Lance, summoning a spear of crystalline ice.

*Utterly pathetic—there's no way that haphazardly cast attack would ever hit me!*

As a knight in his past life, the behemoth has fought against many foes wielding magic. He's faced skilled veterans ever variable in their attacks, employing a refined repertoire of feints as they attacked.

The minotaur has its back to the wall, and there's no way he wouldn't see through its desperate attack spell.

"Meow!"

The behemoth swiftly adjusts the angle of his wings and does a half turn in the air, dodging the Icicle Lance with ease.

"Meow!" *Flame Edge!* The behemoth unleashes the sharpest Elemental Tail Blade in return.

*Slash—!!*

The searing blade of flame slices through the minotaur vertically, lopping it in two perfect halves.

*Hot damn—that's playing with fire. Its edges are perfectly golden brown. Time to dive right in.*

The behemoth chomps down on the well-charred minotaur. As he chews the meat, he finds it close to beef, and umami richness and beef juice fill his mouth.

*Mmm! This is good. I'll definitely regain energy from this.*

The behemoth convenes on stuffing his gullet with all three of the minotaurs, one by one. When he's full, he absorbs the remains with his Storage skill and again starts making his way toward his destination.

---

**Name: None**
**Type: Behemoth (cub)**
**Innate Skills: Elemental Howl, Skill Absorb,**
    **Elemental Tail Blade**
**Absorbed Skills: Storage, Poison Fang, Flight,**
    **Fireball, Icicle Lance**

---

*Dddgggonnn!!!!*

A corner of the labyrinth erupts with a massive boom, and dust floats through the air.

*The earth caved in from one smash…? Golems are the real deal—pure iron brutes.*

Beholding the power of a single golem attack before his very eyes, the behemoth expresses unaffected admiration from within his heart of hearts.

But there's a reason his destination led him back the way he came—to exact revenge on the golem.

*Let's go! Flight!*

Jet-black wings spread from the behemoth's back. He stomps on the ground and rockets into the sky.

The reason the behemoth retreated from the golem previously was due to his lack of reach. Now, after attaining his wings from defeating the wyvern, he is able to fight on even terms.

"Meow!" *Rock Howl!*

The behemoth aims for the golem's weakness, the script engraved on its head, and sends rock hailing toward the earth.

"*Gohhhohhhh!*"

*Crafty bastard!* the golem seems to say as it lifts its arms much faster than its lumbering form would indicate and protects the script on its head from the incoming Rock Howl.

The behemoth clicks his tongue in a suppressed mew and flaps his wings fiercely, distancing himself from the golem's opposite giant arm, which is now coming down at him in a sweeping arc. It passes directly in front of his face.

The behemoth is thrown off balance from the rush of air pressure generated by the strike.

*At this rate, I won't be able to get at it. I need to take down one of its arms.*

The behemoth decides his course of action as he barely averts falling to his death through expert wing control. After this split-second thought, the battle-worn warrior behemoth conjures a battle plan immediately.

"Meow!" *Time for you to die!*

The behemoth rains down the Elemental Howl, Flame Howl, on the golem's arm, which it has refused to remove from protecting the magic script on its head, despite having used the other to lay down a massive swing attack.

The golem's body is made of iron. If the behemoth can't succeed in melting it, the golem will simply step back and swing again with its other arm.

The behemoth evades the attacks and continues to strike—again, again, and again—ripping into the golem's body with Flame Howl. Yet the golem does not drop its defense. Its arm is now red-hot with flame, but it's nowhere close to actually melting.

At this rate, the behemoth's mana and stamina will run dry before he can actually melt the golem's arm off.

*Will this rematch be a failure...?*

Right after thinking that, he decides to activate Rock Howl.

"Meow!" *Rock Howl!*

Massive rocks begin pelting the golem's arm.

And then—the second the rocks make contact, a sharp sound rings out.

*Shakkkinnn!!*

Its arm is clearly dented.

Earth Elemental Howls can't destroy it, and fire Elemental Howls can't melt it. In that case, why not combine the two??

The behemoth's battle plan is to heat up the golem's arm and make it brittle before delivering the telling blow with Rock Howl.

*Rock Howl!*

*Rock Howl!*

*Rock Howl—!!*

The behemoth charges up a Rock Howl before releasing, rinsing, and repeating. Eventually, he succeeds in obliterating the golem's arm.

The golem attempts to protect its head with the remains of its single arm, but it's too late.

After using one last howl, the behemoth accelerates and rushes into close proximity with the golem, twisting his body to fly horizontal with the golem. His tail is sticking straight out, and it's fully formed as a greatsword through Rock Edge—

*Gakkkinnn!*

A vicious, sharp sound erupts. One of the characters of magic script has been completely erased. The golem's red eyes lose their flame, and it begins groaning immensely before falling to the ground.

The behemoth is victorious—

*Okay, so what now?*

The behemoth pauses, staring at the golem's remains. The monster was unequivocally fearsome. Eating from its flesh will provide a most powerful skill.

But its body is absolutely massive—and made of iron. The little beast couldn't chomp through it, no matter how hard he tried.

*Just hold on a second?! I don't have to actually chew it up.*

The behemoth casts his gaze in every direction. And he finds what he's looking for.

A chunk of the golem—ripped off from his final attack. Fortunately, the chunk is not sharp. Swallowing it shouldn't injure his throat.

The behemoth picks up the piece in his jaws and swallows it whole.

*Okay, let's see!*

He casts Status immediately and checks his new skill inventory.

---

**Name:** None
**Type:** Behemoth (cub)
**Innate Skills:** Elemental Howl, Skill Absorb, Elemental Tail Blade
**Absorbed Skills:** Storage, Poison Fang, Flight, Fireball, Icicle Lance, Iron Body

---

His skills have increased, as suspected. The absorbed skill Iron Body... From the name, it must be a defensive skill.

The behemoth tests his new skill immediately.

"Meow!" *Okay! Iron Body!*

His orange tabby fur turns a dark gray, and he can feel his body getting stiff.

*All right then, let's see exactly what effects this has.*

The behemoth begins trotting suddenly. The skill doesn't seem to impede his movement.

*Straight for it!*

The behemoth races directly toward the golem's remains. He's going to tackle it.

*Gakkkinnn!*

The grating, explosive sound of metal on metal.

Although he's rushed full force into the golem's corpse, he isn't damaged in the least and doesn't feel any pain.

*Iron Body...what a great skill. With this at hand, the average monsters' attacks won't leave a scratch.*

The behemoth nods in satisfaction at the high durability Iron Body has granted him.

*Hmm? What's that...?*

After taking down the golem and acquiring a new skill, the behemoth is mewing contentedly as he walks down the path when he spies something ahead.

It's a box made of metal, adorned on every last surface—commonly known as a "treasure box."

Aside from monsters, the labyrinth also generates these boxes, although rarely. Occasionally, they contain powerful weapons or valuable gems, and finding one can possibly lead to a small fortune.

Hunting monsters and buying and selling their raw materials to make a living defines the occupation of an adventurer. The majority of them dream of finding a treasure box and getting rich quick. However, the chances of actually coming across one are extremely low.

The majority of adventurers never actually see such a thing in their lifetimes. The behemoth coming across one is nothing short of a miracle.

*Maybe true, but it doesn't really affect me...*

Even if he finds a powerful weapon or precious gem, the behemoth, having been given a second life, doesn't really have a use for them.

Even so, the behemoth wants to know what's inside and rises up on his hind haunches to push the box open while visibly shaking.

He found the box, and he wants to know what's inside. He can't escape this human curiosity. The box creaks and groans before sliding open.

And inside—

*Hmm. A diamond—what sheer beauty.*

The behemoth is perched on the treasure box's edge, peering inside. The diamond is massive and a vaguely opaque white. Yet even in the dimly lit labyrinth, it's emitting a mystical light.

He probably won't have a use for it, but this is too good to pass up. He'll take it with him as a memento...

The second the behemoth reaches out and touches the diamond...his entire field of vision—no, the entire space surrounding him—starts to shake, and he is stunned.

*What the—?!*

The behemoth determines that he's in danger and quickly turns around to retreat...

*What is happening?! I can't control my own body... What the hell is going on?!*

The twisted anomaly will not let the behemoth go.

Then the distortion morphs into a spiral and sucks the frazzled behemoth deep inside.

*Where...the hell am I?*

Mere moments after being sucked into the spiral, the behemoth stands in an abyss of darkness. The air is completely different from where he was before. A prickling sensation ripples across his skin... He also feels atmospheric pressure.

From these facts, the behemoth knows from instinct that he's been warped to a completely different location. The diamond that he found was no ordinary gem. It was a magic stone—a "Warp Crystal."

These Warp Crystals are a magic item that transport whoever touches them to a completely different place in the labyrinth. They could warp one near the entrance or send whoever touches them down to the lower levels. The destination is random.

Yet the behemoth is certain that, in his case, the results will not be pretty. The reason is the foreboding sense of pressure he's felt on his skin since arriving.

There's no mistaking the fact that a powerful presence lurks nearby. And his instincts tell him that he absolutely must not be discovered by it.

"Just how long do you plan to linger on top of me, vulnerable weakling?"

"—?!"

The steely, thick voice reverberates throughout the room, and every one of the behemoth's hairs stands on end. In the same moment, he's overtaken by the feeling of his body surging up through the air forcefully. In reality, it isn't his footing but *this thing* itself that's rising.

The behemoth loses his balance and is thrown to the ground. It's a good thing his body is flexible. A human would have lost their battle with the fall and been unable to avoid certain injury.

*Wh-what is this thing?!*

The behemoth has finally realized that his footing rested on top of the body of a horrible abomination. Soaring in front of him is a gigantic, hulking form covered in lizard-like, multicolored scales. Its legs bulge with muscle, and razor-sharp claws extend from its feet. Its tail is thicker than a tree trunk and impossibly long. Finally, piercing eyes and a gaping maw that could devour the very essence of life on earth...

It's an earth dragon. There are numerous families of dragons, and this one reigns as an absolute dominator among their highest ranks. It represents the S-ranked monster class.

"You have disturbed my slumber...an offense punishable by death—!!"

Ignoring the behemoth's shock, the earth dragon raises its front legs and brings them down thundering toward him.

Dragons are a proud species. Perching atop one's head is completely unforgivable.

The dragon is ready to lay judgment upon the behemoth and kill him.

In an effort to flee, the behemoth flies into the air...but it's no use. The earth dragon's claw swipes are simply too fast. There's no escaping them.

*Then how about this...?! Iron Body!*

If he can't escape, then he must at least protect himself.

The behemoth activates Iron Body, the skill he just recently acquired from the golem. The earth dragon's metal claws and the behemoth's iron body collide, and a sharp, horrible sound erupts.

*Imbecile...*

The behemoth's eyes are wide in shock. A massive crack has opened across his belly. Although his body is hardened, it still hurts. The surging pain takes control of his body.

The earth dragon twists its maw toward the behemoth, who's still breathing despite taking the normally fatal blow, and praises him.

"Grrrawww...you've taken a blow from my claws and survived. I must compliment you...but this is the end."

The behemoth is rendered immobile from the searing pain. The earth dragon brings its face close to the behemoth and opens its maw. Viscous saliva drips from its mouth... It's clearly planning to devour the behemoth.

*This is the end; this is it...*

The behemoth has an epiphany. No matter how hard he tries to escape, in this current body, he will always be caught.

But he's not going down without a fight!

With the earth dragon's maw gaping wide in front of him, he bares his fangs with a flash.

"Gwahhhahaaaahahhhh?!"

A bloodcurdling cry erupts from the earth dragon. Looking closely, the behemoth sees that blood is streaming from its left eye.

*Heh-heh-heh...that's one blow straight to the dragon's eye.*

The behemoth's face is contorted with pain, but he still manages a satisfied chuckle.

A moment from being devoured, the behemoth activated one of his Elemental Tail Blade skills, Aether Edge. The earth dragon was preoccupied with the wounded behemoth while he inched the invisible blade closer and closer to its face before thrusting right into an eye.

The earth dragon wails and flounders across the room as the behemoth lies down for cover close by. Now all he needs to do is wait for the perfect timing... At least, that's what he thought—

*What...the...hell?!*

A single beam of light illuminates the behemoth.

*The ceiling...the ceiling has been ripped open!!*

The ceiling of the earth dragon's expansive chamber is now sporting a massive hole. Mewing painfully, the behemoth activates his Flight skill. He flaps his wings precariously and somehow manages to take to the air.

But the earth dragon has noticed. It has no intention of letting the behemoth go, and its claws shoot toward its tiny prey.

The behemoth escapes the claws speeding past just below him by the skin of his teeth.

"Youuuuuuuuu—gwaaaaaaarrrhhhh!!"

The earth dragon's bloodcurdling curse reverberates profanely.

Earth dragons are from the earth elemental branch of the dragon family. They have no wings on their backs and naturally cannot fly.

The behemoth has escaped.

"Huff—phew!!"

The behemoth pants as he frantically flees the monsters chasing him. He's managed to slip through the seemingly endless gap that opened up in the ceiling and reach a new layer.

Though he escaped the earth dragon, that wasn't the only danger. Noticing the wounded behemoth, a goblin now gives chase.

It may just be a goblin, but in his pitiful state, a group of them attacking all at once could pose a threat. He presses on...and succeeds in obliterating all the goblins.

*Guh...I'm feeling weak...*

This is the end of the line. The behemoth has lost all stamina and resolve as he collapses in place.

*Gahhh...I might have been so close to finally escaping this labyrinth.*

Goblins litter the new level he's entered above the hole in the ceiling. This tells him that this layer is indeed close to the exit.

Regardless, his body has reached the breaking point. He twists his face in chagrin.

*Thmp, thmp—*

As the behemoth lies in a heap, he can hear footsteps. They're heavy... These footsteps carry the telltale sound of shoes. That means it's a person, and if they're in this place, they must be an adventurer.

*If they find me here, on the verge of death, I will be hunted down for certain...but it doesn't matter. That would still be leagues better than being killed by another monster...*

The behemoth falls unconscious.

Labyrinthos is the name of a high-walled city filled with brick and stone houses in addition to well-maintained roads. It also features aqueducts running throughout its domain, which carry gondolas leisurely gliding here and there. With pilots acting as tour guides, the gondolas are a famous sightseeing activity here.

Yet the city's most notable attraction is not its tourism.

That honor rests with the labyrinth that is the city's namesake. The high walls ringing the city protect the inhabitants from outside invaders, but perhaps more importantly, they also trap any monsters that manage to escape from the depths that lie below. If something in the labyrinth ever went awry, the city would be a very dangerous place indeed. Nevertheless, Labyrinthos is prospering.

Raw materials harvested from monsters plus minerals and medicinal herbs collected from inside the dangerous maze satisfy the citizens' daily need for commodities. Adventurers and merchants alike travel from faraway lands to obtain and hawk these goods.

In one corner of the city, a monster bathed in moonlight awakens in the room of an inn.

*I'm...warm? I can feel something on my skin?*

The behemoth, now awake, is wary of the warm sensation enveloping his entire body. Looking around, he realizes he's on a bed.

*What is the meaning of this? Last I remember, I lost consciousness in the labyrinth...?!*

The behemoth is now even warier of his situation. He wonders if this...is the afterlife? Or perhaps even a dream world?

*If it's a dream, it's a damn comfortable one. This warmth...and that light fragrance...what could this smell be?*

The behemoth is wrapped in a blanket, and a sweet...comforting aroma wafts from it.

*Hmm... Looks like I'm dead after all. In that case, I might as well sleep awhile longer.*

Just as the behemoth starts drifting off again, enveloped by the blend of warmth and pleasant smells—

"Ohhh! I'm so glad you're awake!"

A clear, soft voice—like a lilting bell toll—rings in his ears.

*What the—?!*

Suddenly hearing an unfamiliar voice, the behemoth leaps up from the bed to confirm the source.

*It's...an angel...*

Indeed, he noticed an angel—well, not actually, but a girl so beautiful she could be mistaken for one is standing right there. She has shining platinum-blond hair and cool ice-blue eyes... Altogether, her features impart a kind, gentle affection. With skin as white as porcelain underneath a stark-white negligee, she looks absolutely stunning...

And a part of her body is bouncing up and down. It's her ears! They're long and slightly pointy as they bob. It appears this girl is a demi-human—an elf maiden!

"Shouldn't I be the one who's surprised? I was on a quest in the labyrinth when I stumbled upon you, an adorable kitten, injured and unconscious... Did you get a widdle bit lost in there?"

The behemoth is flabbergasted by the girl's beauty as she addresses him with her lilting voice. Suddenly, she picks him up...

"Meowwwn!"

...and then pulls the behemoth toward her chest in a tight embrace.

*They're...*massive!! *What should I do?! They're perfect apples... No, god, these are* melons!!

There's no doubt—the elf girl's bust is incredible. They're in a category...that can only be defined as melon-scale.

The behemoth is so blown away that any thought he had of resisting has long since been thrown to the wind as he simply acquiesces to her grasp.

"Heh-heh...you don't mind me hugging you, do you? You're a really good boy!"

Looking down at the behemoth pressed between her breasts, the elf girl smiles gently and rubs his head while repeating, "Good boy, good boy."

*Wow...this is beyond amazing. Her soft embrace and this sweet fragrance... Does the smell of the bed all come from her...?*

The behemoth's current situation is what some would call paradise on earth. Despite being a veteran knight at heart, he's been completely won over, willingly surrendering himself to her youthful affection.

As he does, he understands the reason he is currently alive... and that this elf girl saved him... Looking down, he sees that his wound from the earth dragon has mended. It seems likely that the girl used a potion to heal him.

*That means the footsteps I heard in the labyrinth were hers. Given the way I look, it's no surprise she mistook me for a cat.*

The general appearance of a behemoth cub is not well-known information. The elf girl is also unaware.

"Heh-heh, you look so sleepy... Do you want to fall asleep again, with me this time?"

The girl heads toward the bed, still holding the behemoth.

*Sleep...with you...?!*

A mental battle starts to overpower the behemoth. The girl holding him closely is an absolutely stunning beauty. Even in his previous life, he never beheld a girl with such breathtaking looks. That same girl is holding him, and what's more, she wants to sleep with him.

As they fall on the bed, the elf girl embraces the behemoth tightly again.

A sensation of pure, indescribable, unadulterated joy envelops the behemoth's entire being.

*What is...this? It's heaven, I knew it.*

The blissful sensation, her sweet fragrance, and a motherly, loving embrace like none other... The exhausted behemoth naturally falls into a deep sleep, enveloped by the girl's affection.

The next morning—

*　　*　　*

"Good morning, my cute kitty!"

The elf girl calls out sweetly to the behemoth, who has awakened after sleeping the whole night through. She's still hugging him close, just like the night before.

"Meowww."

Upon mewing, the sleepy behemoth uses his cub instincts to burrow even deeper in between her breasts. Yet again, words fail to describe his elation.

This is the pure realm of absolute heaven.

"Heh-heh, you really are a little lover boy. But I'm sorry—I have to get up now."

She releases the behemoth from her embrace and stands up from the bed. The behemoth experiences a moment of regret when her heavenly warmth separates from him, but it soon passes.

"Okay—!!"

The elf girl begins stripping out of her white negligee. Just like yesterday, the behemoth's body is overpowered by her presence. Black—her panties are black. What's more, the total coverage remaining on both her upper and lower half is now very little.

Speaking of lower half, she's wearing a G-string... Her breasts are plentiful, and her waistline is taut and flawless. Her tight rear and hip curves swallow up the strings of her thong...

Any healthy, red-blooded male would be losing his mind.

This girl...even though she looks refined and clean...what is with this slutty underwear? Maybe she's a professional? A neat and tidy, clean professional?

Never mind for now. The behemoth, a noble knight in the previous life, casts his gaze away from her as she begins discarding the negligee.

However—

*My god... Is there a more beautiful human form...?*

The behemoth is incapable of looking away.

The lingerie-clad girl... Her proportions are perfect, her skin utterly smooth white porcelain. A beautiful form, unlike any other...

Before the behemoth can even get sexually excited, his heart is plucked out of his chest from her sheer aesthetic beauty. Just as the behemoth becomes fully enamored with her presence, *it* happens.

"Unnngh...!!"

Her melons drop out and bounce rhythmically—impossibly light and effortless, despite their size. The girl continues to remove clothing from a hook on the wall and changes her attire.

The behemoth can hear her putting on her shirt and the sound of her knee-high socks snapping against her skin...

As her melons continue bouncing around while she changes in the nude, the behemoth, despite his greatest intentions, can't help but feel that he'll go full-bore *behemoth* any second...

Finally finished with her tantalizing nude wardrobe change, the behemoth looks at the girl and remembers. *That's right—from what I heard yesterday, this girl is definitely an adventurer.*

Her shirt's midriff exposes the lowest part of her stomach. Her skirt is extremely short, to facilitate ease of movement, and she finishes off the look with a pair of high boots.

*Damn...her underwear was provocative enough, but this is also purely lascivious.*

Her shirt doesn't leave only her midriff exposed. It also fully exposes her bountiful bosom, what you might call a valley between twin peaks. And her skirt—in addition to being incredibly short, it also exposes the soft lines of her rear every time she moves, bouncing up and down.

She's wearing a knife belt around her waist, equipped with two blades. Finally, she also has small pouches attached to a garter belt on each of her plump thighs.

*Hmm. At first, she looks quiet and reserved, but she's clearly part of the advance guard... Wait, the advance guard?? Could she be one of them??*

From her equipment, the behemoth has ascertained that the girl is a member of the advance guard. But he's not convinced.

And he should be suspicious. How does she expect to maneuver around the world with those melons?

"Okay, I'm ready to go. Now, kitty, I'm going out, but I'll leave the window open so you can come and go as you please. Okay? Oh, that's right! I'll put out some milk for you before I go. I'll just go down to get some from the innkeeper."

The behemoth is stunned, but the girl doesn't notice and leaves the room.

Milk...

The second he hears the word, his stomach growls, *Grrrrllll*—it's downright cute.

After a while, the girl returns with a saucer full of milk.

*Thupp-thupp-thupp-thupp...*

The behemoth drinks from the saucer with gusto.

The girl speaks to him affectionately, saying, "Heh-heh, you must have been hungry!"

After the behemoth finishes a portion of the milk, the girl leaves, saying, "I'll be back!"

The behemoth is now alone in the room.

*That girl saved me when I was injured...and that's not all. She held me close and slept with me and gave me milk. Judging from what she said earlier, if I don't run away from this place, she'll take care of me forever...*

In that moment, the warmth from in between her breasts rushes back into his mind.

*It's decided! I will protect this girl, no—my master! My master is*

*an adventurer, and if I, a behemoth, can manage to guard her in secret, she'll never fall to defeat down in the labyrinth!*

The behemoth has certain conviction.

He will become the knight serving his benefactor and protect her to the full extent of his life span.

*If that's my decision, I can't laze about here! I must follow after her!*

The behemoth leaps from the open window to follow after the girl he's sworn to protect…

As he runs through the city of Labyrinthos, his profile shows the same features it did as a knight in his previous life: unabated pride and valor.

*Ta-ta-ta-ta—*

Moments after leaving through the open window, the behemoth finds the elf girl, thanks to her highly revealing adventurer outfit and unique, sweet fragrance. Even in the busy city streets, finding her is a piece of cake.

"Hey, check this girl out…"

"Oh my god, she's fine as hell. And check out those tits…"

Every single man on the street turns and unintentionally cries out in amazement at the girl's beauty, which is simply a cut above the rest.

*What vile creatures…staring at my master with such lecherous gazes… If we were in the labyrinth, I'd strike you down in an instant.*

The behemoth imagines the worst-case scenario in his mind, conveniently ignoring the fact that he thoroughly drank in the elf girl's immaculate figure while she got undressed to change and enjoyed the feeling of her breasts against his fur.

After following her for a while longer, he sees the girl arrive at an aqueduct. A few gondolas are docked and waiting.

"Hey, Aria. You on another quest today?"

"A fine morning, good sir. Yes, please take me to the labyrinth's vicinity."

A man standing on one of the gangplanks faces the girl—Aria—as he speaks to her. Aria smiles congenially and raises the bronze-colored tag hanging from her chest.

Seeing this, several perverted boatmen relaxing on their gondolas overreact and click their tongues at her. They've definitely schemed to get her on their own boats in the past.

*Wow, my master's name is Aria, is it?! A lovely name for a lovely girl. And it seems that here in Labyrinthos, you can ride the gondolas for free if you have an "adventurer's tag"...*

As the behemoth watches the proceedings unfold, his expression shows pure satisfaction, having learned the name of his master—the girl everyone worships.

Regarding the adventurer's tag he also learned of, all adventurers are fundamentally classified into rank from E to S, with a different mineral denoting that rank.

The specific breakdown is as follows:

**E rank = stone**
**D rank = bronze**
**C rank = silver**
**B rank = gold**
**A rank = platinum**
**S rank = diamond**

As a ranking of strength, this breakdown is slightly loose, but adventurer ranks are treated approximately the same way as monster classifications.

Aria is D rank. In terms of strength…she's just graduated from the novice adventurer stage.

"Okay, Aria, give me your hand…"

"I'm fine. I can get on board myself."

The boatman extends his hand to lift Aria onto the gondola, but she smiles and refuses him, jumping onto the gondola with an effortless leap, landing with a quiet *thump*.

*Hmm. In contrast with her fashion choices, my master is very physically gifted. I'm quite relieved.*

The behemoth sighs in relief.

"Ah-ha-ha-ha-ha-ha…"

The boatman's hand falls on thin air, and he laughs to cover his embarrassment, scratching his head. However, interestingly, he does not look dejected whatsoever.

And he shouldn't be. You see, it's because he didn't miss Aria's bouncing breasts the second she landed on the boat deck.

Men are simplistic, period.

"Okay, Aria, we'll be taking off now."

"Okay! Thank you."

The boatman pushes off with a single stroke of his oar, and the gondola moves forward smoothly. But the behemoth can't be left behind. He leaps onto the gondola, just out of Aria's line of sight, and hides himself in the shadow of a piece of baggage on its deck.

"Haaahhhhhhhhhgh—!!"

A girl's voice reverberates through the labyrinth.

A single knife slash dances toward a goblin, and sanguine blood gushes from its throat. Before the blood hits the ground, Aria rushes off in a flash toward her next kill.

"*Gu-gyahhh—!*"

"*Gi-giii?!*"

Her next targets, two goblins waiting in the rear, let loose cries of terror at Aria's blinding speed. That said, they won't go down without a fight. The goblins grip their daggers and wait for Aria's dash to reach them.

But then—

An instant before she steps in toward them, Aria stops on a dime. Just like that, she puts the knife in her hand back into her knife belt and reaches both hands toward the garter belts wrapped around her thighs.

In the next instant, she brings her hands down in a silver flash of light, and her daggers fly and rip into the goblins' bodies.

""*Gu-gyahhhhhhhhh?!*""

The goblins' screams resound from the immeasurable pain. Two tiny throwing knives, with small rings as their handles, are stuck into the goblins' stomach and shoulder, respectively.

"Kill us!"

The goblins are now in a state of shock from the extreme pain. Aria takes two additional knives from her knife belt and falls upon them. Using the momentum from her dash, she takes a blade in each hand and plunges them into the goblins' hearts, securing her victory.

*What the hell did I just see?*

The behemoth has been closely watching over the fray from the shadows and is stunned. Aria's knife skills include regular and throwing knives, and she's not bad with them, either.

That said, she's still rough around the edges. Put into words, it's like she's just mastered the basics, essentially. The issue isn't with Aria's handling of her weapons but rather her speed.

The speed of her dash.

The speed with which she switches blades.

And the speed with which she draws her knives to strike.

Her velocity is on another plane, in every regard.

*This is truly unfathomable. She must be activating some sort of skill.*

The behemoth begins hypothesizing that Aria's speed is derived from a skill. And he's correct. Aria has a special skill called Acceleration.

For a few minutes after activating this innate skill, all actions performed by the user are sped up.

Aria only has average knife-wielding skills, but the speed she gains from this innate skill allows her to proceed alone through the top levels of the labyrinth (the first sections) and take out the monsters there.

The behemoth now understands the reason behind Aria's highly revealing outfit. It's not a fashion choice but rather a choice to reduce her weight as much as possible in order to maintain speed.

Well…her panties must be a fashion choice…but forget that for now.

"Phew…finally got them all off. The hardest part of a quest isn't taking out the monsters—it's this annoying task."

Aria wipes sweat from her brow and sighs. The corpses of the three goblins she just defeated lie in front of her…and she's cut off all their ears.

Why is this necessary? It's dictated by the Adventurers Guild that monsters are only deemed defeated when one returns a body part as proof.

The goblins she's slain are confirmed as kills by handing in their ears.

*Ohhh...my master, why are you getting those pretty hands dirty for such nasty work...? Dammit, if I could just show you my true form, you'd never have to do such a thing...*

The behemoth, watching from the shadows, is heartbroken that Aria has to sully her hands with the blood of goblins. He has the skill Storage, which he obtained from a slime. If he could just put it on display, he could take their full corpses home, negating the need to cut off their ears.

"Heh-heh. That said, I'm now finally able to take down three goblins at once! I must be almost ready to step foot in the next level of the labyrinth."

Aria sounds delighted as she tucks the goblin ears into her leather pouch.

In the majority of cases, the stronger the monster, the higher the compensation for defeating them and the price that their raw materials fetch. This is the reason Aria looks so pleased knowing she can now move on to more dangerous areas.

*No, my master! Any hesitation will lead to certain death in the labyrinth! A fine lady like yourself should remain satisfied fighting low-level monsters on the top levels!!*

The behemoth is not himself, and this is because the girl he has pledged as his master is threatening to go deeper into the labyrinth, when she does not yet have the required skills.

*Come to think of it, why do you delve into the labyrinth alone, my master...? Entering with two or more is common sense...*

The labyrinth is deadly. In the upper levels, it's quite rare, but there are hordes of goblins that can completely overtake you. If you fall in defeat to a goblin and become captured, it will not be pretty...especially for a young female adventurer.

Goblins are weak, with low life expectancy. On the other hand, they have one strength—their capacity to multiply. Male goblins can conceive with females regardless of species. This means that if a female adventurer is held captive by a horrendous goblin, she will become its nurse mother.

This information is common knowledge. For this reason, it is most common for female adventurers to delve into the labyrinth as a formed party, even in the upper levels.

"But I think I'll hold back for today. I still need to take down one more goblin anyway."

Aria starts moving while the behemoth is still lost in thought. It seems she's given up on plunging down to the next level. He sighs in relief.

After proceeding a bit farther, Aria comes across another lone goblin.

"Acceleration—!!"

Aria immediately activates her innate skill, Acceleration, which boosts her speed. Just as earlier, she moves with quickness untraceable by the human eye and approaches the goblin. Before the creature can slash with its dagger, she pierces its eyeball with her knife and plunges the blade up into its brain.

*Guh?! Is this really what I'm seeing?*

Watching Aria's string of movements, the behemoth notices something. It's the way her chest moves.

When she runs, it's a given that her melons bounce up and down with abandon. This is pure eye candy. But when she approaches the goblin to attack, *something* happens.

When Aria takes her knife from her belt—

In perfect coordination, her melons bounce out of the way, to the side.

When Aria brings her knife down through the air—

Again, her melons bounce out of the way to avoid obstruction.

The behemoth had wondered how Aria planned to attack in close quarters with those bouncing beauties, but now the mystery has been solved.

The reason Aria can attack in close quarters, despite her breasts, is that they can be activated as a three-dimensional object.

The behemoth is floored by this turn of events.

*It's miraculous! My master's bosom contains a sacred power!*

Aria begins dismembering the goblin's ears, still not noticing the behemoth at all.

Just then, as she finishes removing one of the goblin's ears...

"Gi-giii..."

Another goblin appears.

"Another one. I've defeated as many as I planned, but no matter... Bring it on."

Aria has noticed the goblin's approach and grips her knife as she squares up toward it. She's about fifteen feet away.

*No! Haven't you noticed, my master?! That's a—!!*

The behemoth quickly becomes flustered with Aria as she waits for the attack, planning to try out a counter. The reason is that the goblin in front of her is holding a *staff.*

*"Gu-gyahhh!!" Fireball!*

The goblin—no, the shape-shifting goblin mage—casts the low-level fire elemental spell Fireball from its staff.

The fireball sears through the air: *"Gwohhh!"* Aria is completely shocked by this turn of events and is frozen stiff. The second the goblin casts Fireball, the behemoth leaps from the shadows and uses his own Fireball, acquired through Skill Absorb from the minotaur.

*"Meow!" Fireball!*

*Wrrroooosh—!!*

The two fireballs collide in midair and cause a small-scale explosion.

*I'll clean this chump up in no time! Eat my Icicle Lance!*

The behemoth strikes again immediately. The frozen ice spear launches toward the goblin mage and punctures his guts with an icy hiss.

Just as the behemoth delivers the final below, he hears a voice from behind. Of course, it's Aria.

"My...kitty?"

"......"

The behemoth turns around silently. There is no way he can explain this. First and foremost, because he can't even speak.

"It is you, isn't it, my kitty? Why are you here...? And you used magic? Oh my god, can you really be...?!"

"............"

Aria's eyes are welling up as she asks him, and the behemoth can only hang his head in silence.

❖

"Heh-heh, you are so darn cute!"

Just after leaving the labyrinth, Aria addresses the behemoth in high spirits as their gondola sways back and forth. His face is flushed, for reasons he can't explain.

*But why?! Just what is she on about?!*

The behemoth simply cannot comprehend the turn of events. Seeing his master in danger, he leaped in front of her instinctively and activated one of his skills.

When he did, Aria's eyes were wide as saucers. Of course, the behemoth assumed he'd been revealed for the monster he is, the very thought causing him to hang his head in shame.

But in response, Aria said, *"Can you really be...?"*

The behemoth assumed Aria would distance herself from him... but instead...she picked him up and sandwiched him between her breasts in a hug.

*M-master…what are you doing? Aren't you afraid of me now that you know I'm a…monster?*

The behemoth was befuddled. Yet Aria simply said, *"Thank you for saving me…"*

Expressing thanks to the behemoth, at the time balled up perfectly between her breasts, Aria headed toward the exit of the labyrinth, without even batting an eye at the goblin mage's corpse.

Back outside the maze, the boatman cursed the behemoth, seeing him balled up between Aria's resplendent melons.

*Shit!! You little kitten prick; that's where I should be!*

Yet, at the same time, he was also thankful to the behemoth. Stuffed between her breasts as he was, the supple melons were squashed together, looking particularly luscious.

Men are truly complicated creatures, aren't they?

Before long, the gondola reaches the mercantile district of Labyrinthos. Aria expresses her thanks to the boatman and jumps lithely off the boat, with the same grace as when she boarded.

The boatman's voice can be heard trying to reach Aria, saying something like "Perhaps dinner tonight, or…?" but she doesn't hear a word of it, being too entirely involved in rubbing the behemoth's head.

From an outside perspective, it's clear that the boatman was shut down, and his gondolier compatriots all point fingers and laugh.

"Hey, love! Bring me another ale!"

"Heh-heh-heh…what an ass. Let me cop a feel!"

"Hey! Don't even think about it! I'll slap you sideways!"

The Adventurers Guild stands in the center of Labyrinthos's

mercantile district. There's a bar inside where adventurers finished with their day's labor and young female waitresses commonly interact.

The door opens quietly. Normally, all the men inside would lose interest after casting a glance and return to their feasting, but these are not normal circumstances. Why? Because the unrivaled and beautiful elf girl Aria has opened the door.

"Hey, look, it's Aria."

"She looks as good as ever."

"Her tits bounce up and down with every step!"

"Wha—? It looks like she has a cat between them, doesn't it?!"

Whispering voices can be heard coming from seats at the bar.

Since the day Aria arrived in Labyrinthos to become an adventurer, over half the men in the Adventurers Guild have been absolutely obsessed with her.

Witnessing this vulgar chatter, the behemoth's mood turns foul...or so he thought—

*Ahhh...it is soooo warm between my master's breasts...*

The comfort of Aria's embrace and the warmth passing directly into his body from the valley between her twin peaks undermines his awareness.

Even after one night, the behemoth cub yearns for her warmth and cuddles up to her. To that end, even if he wanted to lash out at someone or something, he is completely incapable.

That said, something is about to happen that will awaken the behemoth's dulled senses.

"Wha—? Ha-ha-ha-ha!! Now, just what's this, Aria? Your appearance is blinding me again today."

"Kussman..."

As the speaker approaches Aria with a smile, she lets out a muffled "Oof..."

The man wears light armor over an expertly crafted leather tunic. His comeliness is lower mid-level, at best. He has a bunch of product in his hair, which is slicked back.

Kussman—the son of Labyrinthos aristocrats and just one of many others in love with Aria. Even though he's an aristocrat, he decided to become an adventurer and currently sits at C rank.

He believes that money talks and has attained his current rank by collecting high-quality equipment. He started making advances at Aria a little while back. His lines include, "What do you think—do you want to join my party?"

Most of his approach centers on asking her to join his party. But Aria knows what he's really after—that he doesn't see her as a fellow adventurer but as a girl.

This is obvious through his gaze, which is constantly focused on her cleavage or running up and down from her rear to her legs.

"I'm sorry, Kussman. It's generous of you to invite me, but as I've stated before, I am not interested in forming a party with a man."

"Don't say that, Aria. It's okay—I'll be *gentle* with you."

Kussman reaches out as he says it, going for Aria's waist.

Kussman's behavior makes Aria want to sock him in the face, but she stops in her tracks. He's aristocracy. If she's defiant, she doesn't know what will happen to her.

*This scumbag! How dare you lay a hand on my master!*

In reality, the behemoth is a monster, and matters of this nature don't concern him. Additionally, he's unaware that Kussman is a member of the aristocracy.

The behemoth jumps out from between Aria's breasts, and in that second, Kussman seems to reach right for them—but the behemoth chomps down on his hand.

"Gyaaaa!! What the hell is this cat? Get outta here!!"

Kussman rushes to swat the behemoth away with his free hand.

"Meowwwn!" *This is my chance!*

Just as Kussman lifts his arm to strike—

The behemoth releases his jaw's grip and uses his momentum to leap into the air.

"Kitty?!"

Aria sounds extremely worried, but it's no use. As the behemoth starts tumbling down, he flips over and dives straight for Kussman's face.

His scream resounds through the room. "Waghhhaaaaaaaa—?!"

The behemoth sticks to Kussman's face and scratches him repeatedly.

"You f—!!"

Kussman raises a fist to bring down on the behemoth.

"Meow!" *Nice try!*

There's no chance the battle-worn knight behemoth would take such a pitiful blow. The second before Kussman's punch lands, the behemoth pushes off his nose and artfully flips back onto Aria's chest.

*Crack—!!*

That instant, a sharp sound rings through the bar. Kussman has bashed his fist into his own face—an act of suicidal terror.

"Youuuuuuu mangy rat!! I will tear you to pieces!!"

Kussman spews vitriol as blood gushes from his nose. And in an unbelievable moment, he draws his sword from his waist. He has reached apex rage—intending to kill his assailant.

*Gyah!*

The behemoth's face freezes. But what to make of this situation? His gaze is fixed...on something *behind* Kussman.

"Now, young Kussman, what do you think you're doing, drawing your sword inside the guild?"

The voice reverberates to the deepest psychological core of everyone in the room, as if it were speaking directly to each individual's consciousness.

"You…just… Who…um…?"

Kussman turns slowly and trepidatiously. Deep-seated fear is etched into his expression.

*It's…a…a ghost!*

The behemoth attempts to process what he's seeing.

"Anna!"

Amid the fray, Aria's face is the only one lighting up.

"Aria, are you okay?"

"Yes, as you can see, I'm fine."

"Yes, it seems as much, thank goodness… And now for you, Kussman—are you going to say anything? Depending on what it is, you might end up earning yourself a new asshole, so be careful, okay?"

"Ahhhhhh—!!"

Threatened by the individual who's appeared, Kussman shrieks from the depths of his soul.

And for good reason. The figure in question…is a bona fide monster, no question. Aria called him Anna…but his real name is Arnold Holzweilzenegger.

His six-foot-plus towering frame is covered from head to toe in bondage gear, and atop the neck extending from his gimp suit emerges a skinhead geezer's face covered in technicolor face paint. While this character's actual role is that of receptionist, he (she?) is nevertheless a formidable B-ranked adventurer.

He wields high-level ice magic at will and, during his heyday, was a true abomination, preferring to be called by his second name, "Ice Queen Anna."

Of course, her (his?) hobbies are extremely peculiar. Whether guy or girl…well, that's all beside the point, because anyone who misbehaved within the confines of the guild could expect to be quickly reprimanded with the menacing phrase, "I'll bury you."

…That's the type of person they're dealing with here.

"U-uh...I w-was just showing off my sword to Aria! Ah! And I've just remembered, I had an important meeting scheduled. I'll be on my way, then!"

*Seems like he has experience getting reprimanded?!*

The color drains from Kussman's face as he hastily strings together lies and excuses before skittering out the door.

"Unbelievable. Rushing off in a huff. He deserves a good licking."

Arnold is struck with disbelief as he sighs deeply.

"Thank you so much, Anna. You really helped me out."

"Aria, not a problem, honey. If you're ever in trouble, don't hesitate to let me know."

"Okay!"

*Hmph... Just who is this Anna character? He looks absolutely absurd, but it appears he's close with my master. And he's of solid character, from what I can see.*

The behemoth was wise beyond his years in his past life, and he would never portend to judge the content of someone's character based on their looks. Anna's conversation with Aria, the fact that he saved her, and above all else, reading her tone and expression, the behemoth has decided that she (he?) is a good person.

"At any rate, what's with the cat? He's quite the piece of work, isn't he? He protected you from getting groped by Kussman, right? He's like a knight in shining armor!"

*Hmm. So Anna was watching the whole time. Rather, the fact that he saw through my monster appearance almost immediately is...certainly formidable.*

As the behemoth ponders the situation, Anna stares deeply into his eyes and winks subtly.

"Yes, and that's not the only reason he's special. In the labyrinth earlier, I was overtaken by a goblin that could cast magic, and when I had my back to the wall, he used a magic skill to protect me!"

Oh no! Tension runs through the behemoth's body.

It doesn't appear Aria has any aversion to the fact that he's a monster. Yet if anyone else finds out, he could...likely be killed.

"A magic skill...you say?"

Hearing Aria's claim, Arnold looks suspiciously at the behemoth.

And then...

"A cat...that uses magic...and he has orange tabby fur... Could he be—?"

*I'm finished...*

The behemoth is convinced he's done for.

"—an elemental cat?"

*Yes, yes, that's right. I'm whatever that's supposed to be.*

The behemoth expected Arnold to claim he could be a monster. But instead, he used the term *elemental cat*, a term he's never heard before.

"Do you think so, too? Oh, that's great! I was sure of it!" Hearing Arnold's opinion, Aria can't conceal her glee.

In this world, there exists a very rare creature called an elemental cat. They are more intelligent than normal cats, and in some instances, they can even understand human speech.

They have one other major attribute that differs from normal animal species—they can wield elemental magic.

These animals, due to their intelligence, will become attached to the human they claim as master and, due to their strength, will always attempt to protect that master.

Having saved Aria's life in the labyrinth, the behemoth now worships her as his master and has followed her, using two different elemental magic skills to protect her when she fell into danger.

In summary, Aria doesn't think the behemoth is a monster but has rather confused him for a young elemental cat.

*Hmm, uh-huh... Now that I recall, elemental cats do have the same orange tabby pattern that I do...*

Remembering this, the behemoth begins to feel weak.

"I've decided that his name will be Tama! And from now on, I'll officially raise him as my pet."

Ignoring the fact that Tama is slumped over, Aria announces her decision in a shrill voice.

*What's this?! This must mean that, from now on, I can brazenly follow my master and accompany her anywhere?!*

The behemoth's eyes are shining with delight.

"Hey, Aria—are you sure about that? When elemental cats grow up, they're about six feet long, and they can also crossbreed with other species, so he might even assault you when he's in heat!"

"What are you talking about, Anna? That's *exactly* what I'm hoping!"

*...Oh dear... So that's what Aria had in mind all along...*

Hearing Aria, Arnold has nothing else to add, looking slightly disturbed. In other words, what Aria wants is... No, let's leave that alone for now.

"Tama...hurry up and get bigger, okay? And then someday, you can be my first... Heh-heh, then we'll go *meow, meow* a lot together, okay?"

Aria's face is beet red as she...she kisses the behemoth—Tama—on the head.

*Shiver.*

A sensation he's never felt before surges through Tama's entire being.

"Okay, Aria. I need to get back to the receptionist counter. You've come to the guild to declare your goblin quota, no?"

"Yes, that's right. I'm sorry—I got excited..."

Aria had been staring heatedly at Tama, fit snugly between her breasts, and finally looks back up at Arnold as he speaks to her. As if in apology, she reaches down and strokes Tama's head ever so lovingly. Maybe it's just his imagination, but her caress is even more sensuous than the night before.

*Master...did you really mean what you just said earlier? No— there's no way a young, innocent girl like my master could be... Dammit! What the hell does* go meow, meow *mean?*

Tama is soliloquizing ad nauseam regarding what Aria said about *you can be my first...*

"Well then, go ahead and bring out your proof."

"Okay. Here you go—"

As Tama anguishes over Aria's words, Aria and Arnold have moved to the reception desk, where they're confirming that Aria has met her quest requirements.

Aria removes from her leather pouch the goblin ears she cut off and lines them up on the counter.

"Two, four, six...okay. I confirm ten ears from five goblins. This completes your quest. I'll assess their condition and prepare your payment, so take a seat on the bench or go ahead and kill some time in the bar like always, sweetie."

Aria smiles at Anna and replies, "You got it, Anna."

Arnold's words—*assess their condition*—mean that the monster parts brought back from a quest can be assessed for buying and selling as raw materials, on top of the payment for defeating the goblins themselves.

Monster skin is used in a number of daily commodities and, depending on the type of meat, often as food. Other applications are also possible, including monster materials used as ingredients in healing potions and more.

In this case, the part that will be repurposed as raw material is the skin of the ears. Goblin skin can be used for wallets or weapon handles, as well as scabbards—there are many different applications.

Assessment involves a professional appraiser in the back of the guild who decides if the materials retrieved will fetch value on the market or not.

"Okay, what should we do until the assessment is finished? I'm a little hungry for an afternoon snack, so relaxing in the bar for a bit could be nice…"

Aria puts her finger to her lip and looks perplexed.

Just at that moment…

"Hey, Aria, come have a drink with us, eh?!"

"Heh-heh, yeah, we'll buy you a drink!"

A group of male adventurers drinking in the bar surrounds Aria with mugs of ale in hand.

*Hmph… Again, eh? My quests always end like this.*

Aria sighs quietly to herself, covering the fact that she's quite annoyed inside.

Aria is very fond of the food served in the bar attached to the guild. If possible, she would eat here every day. However, as of now, she's unable to do so due to the throngs of men crowding around her with their best pickup lines.

"I'm sorry; I appreciate the invite, but I have business to attend to after this…"

Aria gently refuses their advances with what seems like a reasonable excuse.

"Oh, I see. Well, maybe next time…"

The men don't pursue Aria that aggressively this time. After all, the world's toughest, macho receptionist girl (?) is waiting close by. They're especially hesitant now, after seeing how pathetic Kussman looked minutes ago.

*Hmm. It seems my presence is also a strong deterrent to these pieces of filth approaching my master. I'll continue to drive them away zealously.*

Tama is sending a sharp glare out from between Aria's breasts, nodding contentedly at the spooked looks of the men in the room.

"Ah, what can I do? I guess I'll wait here on the bench again... Heh-heh, but starting today, Tama is with me, so I don't need to be sad, right?"

"Meowww—"

Although Aria looks disappointed for a moment, the second she peeks down at Tama snuggling in her cleavage, she smiles broadly.

Tama mews loudly in response, to say, *Of course! I would never let you become sad, my master!*

A few minutes later—

"That's right! Good boy!"

"Meow!" *S-stop, please, master...*

Tama has been turned on his back on Aria's knee as she sits on the bench, and she's rubbing his furry tummy to her heart's content.

"Heh-heh...your tummy is so soft and cute, and down *there* is soft, too!"

"Meow—!!" *Yelp!! Master, that's my...*

"It's so squishy—!"

"Meow-gwhaaaaaa—!!"

Tama's cry resounds throughout the entire guild.

"Wow, it's already early evening..."

"Meowr—"

The main street of the mercantile district is dyed bright orange. Aria walks among the commotion of people out shopping for groceries for dinner, Tama tucked between her breasts.

The item assessment was very busy today, and Aria ended up waiting for quite some time. Tama was subjected to belly rubs—and rubs somewhere that shouldn't be mentioned—the entire time, and his voice has lost all energy.

"What to do for dinner…? Going into another restaurant and getting hit on will be a hassle. Let's buy something and go home. Elemental cats are omnivores, if I recall, so let's get something for you, too, Tama!"

"Meow!"

Hearing this, the exhausted Tama's vitality is restored. Because he was reborn as a monster, he thought he'd have to go his entire lifetime without another chance to eat human food.

"Hey, Aria! Want to take home some shish kebab skewers from my shop? I just grilled 'em!"

"No, no—you need some spare rib from my shop! I'll give you a special price, Aria."

As Aria walks along the street, the open-air shop owners all call after her in competition. Some of them openly ignore the customers they were just helping… Aria's popularity is obvious.

"Wow, everything looks so good! Okay, I'll take five skewers—chef's choice—and two orders of the spare rib."

"Okay!"

"Thank you always!!"

The shop owners are elated with Aria's orders as they pack them up for her. They're totally overdoing it—including over double what she actually asked for in the order.

"That's so much… Thank you, as always."

"Not at all! Don't even worry about it."

"That's right—you're a regular, Aria. And oh, it seems today you have a supercute kitty with you, don't you?"

Aria is overjoyed at their kind treatment and the extra food as she thanks them. The shop owners force ungainly smiles her way.

The shop owner who sold the spare rib looks at Tama...but Tama's already onto him—onto the fact that he's pretending to look at Tama, but he's really leering at Aria's cleavage.

*This bastard... Does he really want to meet the same fate as those before him?*

Tama's thoughts are disturbed as he waits, feline rear twitching back and forth, ready to pounce—when something happens.

"Oh no. Both my hands are full now—I won't be able to hold you, Tama... Oh, of course! On the way home, make sure to stay still and quiet, okay?"

With that, Aria picks up Tama and—*shoop*—slips him right between you-know-where.

*Wh-what the hell?!*

Both shop owners' bodies are gripped by a hair-raising shudder.

Her valley between twin peaks...yes...her cleavage.

Tama's body is tightly squeezed in between Aria's ample bosom, with only his head peeking out. Tama keeps his body stiff, shocked at this turn of events.

Overwhelmed by the visual appearance of a kitten staring at them from between that valley, the two shop owners can only stand gobsmacked, swallowing their saliva.

"Okay, if that's all, we'll be on our way now."

The shop owners have gone stiff as two boards, and Aria looks at them quizzically before placing a few copper coins down for payment and leaving.

"Hey, shish kebab."

"What's up, spare rib?"

"I...wish I was born a cat..."

"You're telling me!"

*Ahhh…this place is truly heaven…*

Having returned to the inn, Tama can't stop thinking this, even after he's released from between Aria's breasts. Warm, fuzzy, cuddly sensations rack his body with each step. As an added bonus, Aria was a bit sweaty after finishing her quest and secreted more of her sweet fragrance than usual, inviting Tama to doze off and lose himself in her.

"Okay, Tama, come here. Let's eat together."

"Meow-ow!!"

Aria lines up the food she purchased on the table in the room. The sauces and spices attack Tama's olfactory sense, and his stomach growls.

He leaps in a single bound onto the table, and Aria grabs a skewer, pointing it toward him while saying, "Open wide!"

*Chomp—!* Tama hasn't eaten anything since the milk this morning, and he rips into the skewer with abandon. The meat, cooked over charcoal, is rich, delicious, and incredibly juicy. The sweet and spicy sauce fills his mouth.

*This is what I'm talking about!*

How long has it been since he had real food? Overly excited, Tama devours an entire skewer in one bite.

"Heh-heh, you're really going to town… Eat as much as you want and get bigger soon, okay…?"

Aria looks at Tama enthusiastically, but this time, she lets him prioritize chowing down on the meat.

"Tama, you helped me in the labyrinth, and what's more, you're an elemental cat… I was so lucky today. I think I'll have a drink to celebrate."

Tama is now tearing into the spare rib. Aria stands and retrieves a bottle from the corner of the room. Judging from the label, it's fruit liqueur.

In this kingdom, men are recognized as adults at age fourteen and women at age twelve. Aria looks like she's about fifteen or sixteen years old. That means she's a full-fledged adult.

*Hmm. Master. Should a young girl really be drinking by herself? Wait—I guess it's vastly preferable to her going out for a drink and letting some smug bastard try to have his way with her.*

These are Tama's thoughts as he watches a drop of the fruit liqueur spill from Aria's mouth into her ripe, busty valley.

"Heh-heh, I feel so good…"

Aria has the liqueur bottle in one hand, her eyes now vacant. There are three empty bottles on the table… This is overdrinking. She must be absolutely overjoyed to have Tama as her pet.

In this moment, Tama has gotten sick of drunken Aria and decided he can't watch any longer. He's on the bed, grooming his fur with his tongue.

"Tama, how can you leave your master all by her lonesome and endlessly lick yourself? You've gone cold… If you keep that up, I won't take you to the bath with me, got it?!"

*The…bath…?!*

Tama stops dead in his tracks at words he cannot ignore.

Aria dismisses him for now and starts cleaning up the empty bags on the table before putting a change of clothes and a towel into a basket beside the bed.

"If you're coming along, now is the time!"

Aria looks at Tama with forlorn eyes and pushes the basket toward him.

*It means…If you're coming, get in this basket*, he surmises.

*Thi…this cannot be helped. I am my master's knight. I cannot*

*leave her side, for what if something should happen to her, at times unexpected? There is no choice in this matter!*

As a proud knight, entering the women's bath is a preposterous proposition. However, he has reason to assume that the unmatched beauty who is his master *could* be assailed by a man incited by carnal desire at any moment. In that case, he must let go of his pride and escort his master…

Tama forces himself to agree with this rhetoric and hops into the basket…without a care and light as a feather.

"Hey there, Aria. Down for a bath?"

"Yes. It's a bit later, but can I still use it?"

Descending the stairs from the second floor, Aria engages in conversation with a woman carrying a tray of food.

The second floor of the inn houses all the guest rooms. The first floor includes reception and a bar. The woman Aria is speaking to is the proprietor of the establishment.

"Sure, that's not a problem. You'll be the last one in. Take your time, sweetie. And go ahead and wash your kitty really well, too."

"Thank you very much!"

Aria expresses thanks at the proprietor's congeniality before heading toward the back of the inn. Guests take turns using the washroom, but it's big enough to include a large washing area and tub.

One of the men in the bar sees Aria heading for the bath and starts following her, but the proprietor shoves a fist toward him and stops him in his tracks.

*They're…they're floating…*

In the changing room, Tama is again watching Aria's enchanting clothes-changing ritual. Then he gets the satisfaction of scrubbing Aria down in the washing area.

Aria's physique is absolutely flawless, but on top of that, her skin is without wrinkles—truly a perfect body. Nonetheless, something happens in front of Tama's very eyes that nearly makes him forget this sight.

They're floating. Aria's melons are floating like two buoys out to sea in the bathtub. Tama floats in the tub, too, absolutely overtaken by this splendorous sight.

"Tama…?"

"Meowr?"

Drunk and perfectly warm in the bath, Aria is staring blankly at the ceiling before suddenly speaking to Tama. He replies, seemingly in haste. He is now fully self-aware of just how deeply he'd been enraptured by the ridiculous scene in front of him, the beauty of Aria's body and the fact that her massive breasts are floating in the water.

"Tama…will I get stronger?"

"…Meow?"

Hearing Aria's question and seeing her eyes shuddering with insecurity, Tama mews worriedly. Aria continues opening up to him.

"There was a demon army invasion in the kingdom I used to live in. At the time, I was so small and couldn't fight. I just hid from everything for as long as I could…but demons have really good noses, and they found me quickly…"

Aria recalls how she felt at the time, and her whole body shudders—but only for a split second. After the moment passes, a smile spreads across her face.

"But in that moment, a Sword Saint appeared...! They were dual-wielding blades in both hands and appeared before me, slashing every one of the demons to pieces. They saved my life."

*Sword Saint...could she really be talking about that Sword Saint?*

Tama knows of the Sword Saint of whom Aria speaks... Some years before, a demon army invasion overwhelmed a certain kingdom, and from out of nowhere, the Sword Saint appeared and slaughtered every last one of them, saving the kingdom, according to the legend that the elf girl Aria is referencing.

Aria was saved by this mysterious Sword Saint. She continues:

"Then I made a decision. Someday I will become as strong as the Sword Saint, capable of helping others when they're in need... That's why I started practicing with knives and became an adventurer to study as an apprentice."

*My master...*

Tama is struck deeply in his heart by the noble way Aria is leading her life.

"However..."

Stopping suddenly, Aria looks despondent and submerges half her face. Tama has a pretty good idea what she wants to say next.

Even though she'd like to help as many people as possible, just today, she was set upon by a goblin, although it was a sudden shape-shifting type, and Tama saved her. Tama assumes that is absolutely mortifying for her.

*It's okay, master... You are still young. With your mettle, you will definitely get stronger! And you have me with you. Until you become much, much stronger, I will stop at nothing to protect you with my life.*

Seeing Aria become despondent, Tama pledges again from the bottom of his heart to protect her for as long as he lives. He skillfully swims to Aria's side and climbs up onto her shoulder, careful not to scratch her skin with his claws before rubbing his face into her cheek lovingly.

"Tama...hee-hee, you are such a sweetheart."

Thanks to Tama, a bright smile returns to Aria's face.

In this moment, a young girl and a behemoth cub have deepened their bond.

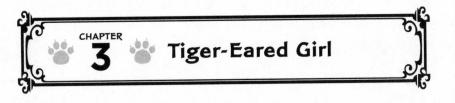

In a corner of Labyrinthos's mercantile district, there lies a shop named Vulcan's Outfitters that purveys items to adventurers. Most of their stock isn't particularly flashy, but the establishment has a reputation for inexpensive goods that are easy to use and highly functional.

Vulcan's Outfitters has another customer today.

"Meow! Hey now, welcome!"

As the door to the entrance opens, a lively voice accompanies a woman emerging from the back. She looks a bit young…what they call "Lolita-faced," and her hair is short and a dark golden. Feline ears, the same color, protrude above. Her skin is the color of sun-kissed wheat, and she's wearing overalls and an apron—but nothing else. It's very eye-catching.

Her breasts are more than ample, exposing both cleavage and side boob and healthy underarms… Her golden-wheat-colored skin is just a bonus.

Her name is Vulcan, and she's part of the tiger-eared race. She might look cute, but she's the owner and proprietor of Vulcan's item shop.

"Hey there, Vulcan. It's rare for you to be here in the early afternoon, isn't it? Aren't you heading into the labyrinth today?"

With a voice like a tinkling bell, the person speaking to Vulcan is…a platinum blonde, hair shining like gold dust. Her elf ears peek out from behind her hair, and she has ice-blue eyes. Her bosom is ample, almost beyond belief, and a small animal is nestled right between them…

Of course—it's Aria and Tama!

Vulcan says, "Meowr, Aria! There was a special blacksmithing order today, so I had to take a break from my adventuring. But I'm finished now, so…maybe I'll head into the labyrinth right meow!"

Looking closely, she has a silver tag hanging on her chest. Vulcan is a blacksmith as well as a C-ranked adventurer.

There are some blacksmiths who personally brave the labyrinth's depths to procure raw materials, and Vulcan is one of them.

"By the way, Aria, you must be here for maintenance on your weapons? And what's with the cat…?"

"That's right. My knives went dull after my quest yesterday. And this is my cat, Tama. He's my pet since yesterday—an elemental cat kitten."

Aria confirms her business and introduces Tama with pride. They're here to tune up Aria's knives, just as she said.

The reason it's already afternoon is that Aria drank too much yesterday and couldn't get out of bed this morning.

"Meow! An elemental cat! That's so rare! Aria, can I hold him a second?"

"Of course you can. Tama, this girl is Vulcan, and she always takes care of my weapons at this shop. Don't scratch her or anything, okay?!"

Vulcan looks at Tama restlessly. She wanted to hold him the second she laid eyes on him. Aria readily consents and cautions Tama before passing him over onto Vulcan's chest.

Tama mews, as if to say, *Absolutely*. It's obvious that Aria and

Vulcan are quite close. In that case, he needs to be close with her, too!

Not to mention, the only people Tama attacks are the injurious lechers who perv after Aria.

*B-bounce—!!*

Landing on Vulcan's chest and being cuddled, Tama's body bounces up and down. They're not as big as Aria's, but they're still giant breasts.

Elasticity and softness... Not to mention, her breasts, exposed by the overalls, impart body heat directly to Tama, and it feels amazing.

"Meowr—he's so calm and cute!"

"Right? I can't believe such a cute kitty became my pet—it's like a dream!"

*The one living a dream is me. Getting scooped up by a noble girl like you, master, and being spoiled absolutely rotten... I cannot be thankful enough.*

Even being cuddled by Vulcan and dandled on her breasts, Tama's deep thankfulness to Aria is renewed. And in the same moment...

*That said, this is truly a comfortable place to be. My elf master, fresh and clean, and the vigorous, beast-like lady Vulcan... Just watching these two beauties engage in friendly conversation is a sight for sore eyes, but being passed back and forth between their embraces and feeling their soft, delicate touch...*

Tama is blown away by it all before he even has a chance to be overcome with arousal.

"By the way, Vulcan. I have something I'd like to ask you..."

As Tama is wrapped up in Vulcan's soft warmth, Aria starts talking like she's just remembered something.

"And what's that, Aria?"

"Actually, I was hoping that…you could make some special defensive equipment for this little guy here."

"Cat armor, huh…? Oh, that must mean you're planning on taking him along on your adventures?!"

"That's exactly right!"

Aria is here for a different reason today—to ask about getting Tama's special protective equipment. She understands that Tama will continue to follow her on her quests, in order to protect her. If that's the case, then she needs to reduce the danger he faces, and her idea is to commission a piece of armor that will protect his body.

In this world, it isn't particularly rare for adventurers to have bonds with animals, fighting alongside them. In some cases, people decide to give their animal partners equipment that doesn't restrict their movement.

*Master!! You really care that much about me…?!*

Tama is once again floored by how much Aria thinks of him, feeling deeply grateful.

He's succeeded in becoming Aria's pet (knight), but because he's been mistaken for an elemental cat, he'll only be able to take advantage of the elemental skills he has, despite acquiring many others.

That means he can't use the defensive skill Iron Body to act as a shield for Aria. But if he has defensive gear—that's a different story. As her knight, he'll be able to become his master's shield.

Well, if it comes to that, that's not all that will be required of him…

"A special piece of animal equipment… I've never made one, but it sounds fun! In that case, he's definitely going to grow up fast, so I'll need to use size-adjusting magic! What will the mold look like…?"

Upon hearing Aria's request, Vulcan picks up a parchment note-pad nearby and starts jotting down the necessary requirements.

Vulcan's trial-and-error production goes long into the night.

The next day—

"Heh-heh, good morning, Tama!"

Once again today, Tama has awoken between Aria's breasts as she speaks to him lovingly.

"Meowr—"

Tama wakes up and rubs his face against Aria's cheek—she loves when he does it. He serves his master, so doing something that she loves is a given... At least, that's what he tells himself when he's constantly rubbing up against her—typical Tama.

"Tama...you're such a lover boy. But I'm glad you're not shy about it. You can love me all you want."

Whenever Tama starts getting affectionate, Aria praises him, perpetuating the cycle.

*Phew...this is exceptional.*

Having a beautiful girl adore him and being able to love her all he wants—Tama feels euphoric in both heart and body.

*Okay, I have to answer her every beck and call. What clever way can I please her today?*

Having decided as much, Tama springs into action. First, he stops rubbing his face into Aria's cheek. She looks at him with chagrin, as if to say, *Are you finished...?* And then...

*Lick—*

Tama gives Aria's elf ear a single lick.

"Ahhhn—!"

*Wha—? This is not the reaction I imagined!*

Aria's voice is erotic, and Tama reflexively pulls his head back.

Aria's cheeks are flushed pink. Her breathing becomes a bit rough, and she rubs her thighs together.

With hazy eyes, she says...

"Tama...more..."

And—

*Oh god! I've flicked a switch in her! Is my master really into that? She's not an elf—she's a nymph!*

Tama jumps off the bed and retreats to the corner of the room. Aria stands up shakily and approaches him ever so slowly.

She's mumbling to herself, saying, "Tama, I didn't know you knew that technique" and "I don't think I can wait for you to grow up and get bigger..."

*This is no good! I'll get eaten alive!*

Tama's instincts are blaring. Aria corners him and scoops up his tiny body. Yet, in the next moment, the hand of his savior comes to the rescue.

*Knock-knock*—someone is at the door.

"Y-yes?!"

Aria almost seemed like she had hearts floating in her ice-blue eyes, but thanks to the sudden appearance of a visitor, she's returned to her senses.

"It's me-ow—Vulcan!"

"Vulcan?! I'll o-open the door; just a second!"

Aria hurriedly fixes her posture. She wasn't sure if she should answer the door in her negligee, but they're both girls, and she doesn't want to keep Vulcan waiting, so she heads to the door.

"Meowr, sorry it's so early! But I really wanted you to see *this* right meow! So I'm here."

"Ah! Is this…?"

"Yep, it's Tama's special defensive equipment! It was so much fun to make, I ended up staying up all night."

Vulcan holds a tiny piece of armor in her hand. Aria's face lights up when she sees it.

*Phew…it seems that master's interest has shifted to the gear. Nice one, Vulcan!*

Tama sighs in relief.

Come to think of it…creating armor in such a short amount of time is altogether unrealistic, but there's a reason behind it.

The majority of the blacksmiths in this world have special blacksmith skills that have the capacity to increase the speed with which they can forge items or imbue a target with heat energy, among many other abilities.

These skills are the reason Vulcan has found so much success as a blacksmith at such a young age.

"Tama, let's try it on you right away!"

"Meow!"

As Aria takes the equipment from Vulcan and spreads it open, Tama mews eagerly and pushes his legs through the openings.

And then…

"Oh yes, it's so cute!"

"Meow, I'm so glad I could make it without any problems!"

Peering down at Tama in his defensive equipment, Aria feels her cheeks flush, and Vulcan nods in satisfaction. The body of Tama's gear resembles leather armor, and it has steel protective plates in several spots on the top. Vulcan explains that it's made this way so it doesn't restrict Tama's nimble movement.

The headpiece of the outfit is a helmet fashioned from wood and steel. It has ear holes so that it won't impair Tama's hearing.

It makes Tama look like he's cosplaying as an adventurer, and it's adorable. Aria loves cats to begin with, and for her, this is a whole new level of cute.

"Tama, you can move around just fine, right?"

"Meow-ow!"

Tama answers Vulcan's query regarding his capacity to move with gusto and turns in a circle to show her.

*Hmm. It's a bit heavy, but since I'm a behemoth, this shouldn't be a problem. According to what Vulcan said yesterday, it has size-adjusting magic cast on it, so I'll be able to wear it for a long time even as I grow.*

Tama is satisfied with the result. This is truly a handmade work by a thriving blacksmith.

"I also came to deliver this!"

Vulcan brings out two knives—she's completed the maintenance on Aria's knives, too.

"Thank you so much, Vulcan."

"Meowr—it was fun to work on a rewarding project for the first time in a while! Okay, well you already paid me yesterday, so I guess I'll be on my way."

Vulcan leaves the two, and on her way out, she lets out a short yawn—she really must have worked all through the night.

"Tama, once we finish breakfast, let's go straight to the guild and take on a new quest!"

"Meow!"

The first layer of the labyrinth, toward the back—

Aria spots a gang of enemies and starts sprinting while activating her innate skill, Acceleration. Thanks to the effect this skill grants, Aria takes advantage of the boost in speed and closes the gap in no time.

"Do-gwah!"

There are five goblins lying in wait, and Aria flies into their midst, landing a kick to one of them, blasting it backward.

"Haaaa-ahhh!"

Aria screams zealously and does a flip in the air, bringing her twin knives down into the throats of two other goblins staring, dumbfounded. Then she springs to the rear, bearing down on the goblin backed against the wall, unable to move.

"Gi-gya—!!"

It should be screaming after what happened to its comrades.

The last two goblins finally read the situation and rush toward Aria. But—

"Meow!" *Icicle Lance!*

A cute mew is heard from the spot where Aria started. A frozen ice spear flies forth, following the voice's path, and pierces both goblins' chests.

Of course, it was Tama.

"Gu...gya..."

The goblins' eyes are wide with anguish. Soon they lose their strength and crumple to the floor in a heap, breathing their last.

"Way to go, Tama! That makes thirty goblins!"

"Meow-wn!!"

After defeating all the enemies, Aria smiles broadly, and Tama mews with glee, following suit.

After receiving Tama's defensive equipment from Vulcan, Aria and Tama headed into the labyrinth as planned. At first, Aria hesitated about how to fight alongside Tama (who she assumed was an animal). However, after fighting a few skirmishes together, she realized that Tama can protect himself with magic skills, as well as provide her cover.

After a few more battles, Aria naturally became the vanguard, while Tama took up the rear guard.

*Mmm! I'm so glad my master is sharp as a tack. Although I'm a behemoth, I'm still a cub and can't keep up with her speed, and because she thinks I'm an elemental cat, I can't use Flight or my Elemental Tail Blade, either.*

As a knight pledging to protect Aria, he was nervous about only using elemental magic, but thanks to the fact that Aria quickly understood his disposition, he can now protect her without wasting any energy. Tama is quite relieved by this turn of events.

"Tama, since we've come this far, don't you want to go down another layer? It shouldn't be a problem if I have you with me, and I think it will be great training for me."

"Meow!"

She proposes the idea to Tama after removing all the goblin ears, and he replies emphatically and nods.

*"Buwhohohooh—"*

Moments after pushing into the second level of the labyrinth, something appears before Aria and Tama—emitting bloodcurdling cries, nearly six feet tall, featuring bloodshot eyes and an upturned nose like a pig... The creature before them is an orc—a swinelike humanoid monster.

It looks incredibly agitated. Perhaps there's a reason—much like goblins, orcs can also conceive offspring with human females.

"Oof...that hideous face strikes fear in my heart..."

Seeing the orc's twisted face, Aria rubs her arms. They're covered in goose bumps. She's likely imagined the worst-case scenario.

Although Aria does have a desire to "go meow, meow" with a grown-up Tama, there's no chance she'd ever consider doing that with an orc.

*"Snooort—"*

The orc is enraged at Aria's reaction and lets out a war cry different from before. It brings up the massive hatchet in its hand and starts loudly stomping toward Aria.

*Whoosh—!!*

The orc brings its weapon down at Aria.

But—

"Too slow!"

Aria sidesteps casually and easily evades the blow by a wide margin.

"Meow!" *Fireball!*

Tama quickly activates a magic skill.

The fireball rips through the room with a rush and lands squarely in the orc's face. It screams from the intense pain of having its face burned and loses its weapon.

"Nice one, Tama!"

This is too good of a chance to miss. Aria closes the distance between the orc and her and jumps into the air. She's holding her knife in the opposite hand and brings it down, aiming for the heart. Yet then she kicks the orc in the stomach to create space between them again.

This is because the struggling orc suddenly brought a fist down toward her. It whiffs through the air. In the same instant, all light goes out of the orc's eyes, and it crumples in a heap.

"Phew…"

Aria sighs deeply. She's only taken down small monsters like goblins and slimes so far. She was super nervous facing the orc, many times her size and much more powerful.

"Heh-heh…this was possible thanks to you, Tama!"

"Meow!"

Aria smiles at Tama, who supported her with perfect timing, and he mews as if saying, *Don't even worry about it!*

*Okay then, we've taken down an orc. It's been a while since I took a bite out of a monster. It might have a skill that I can obtain.*

Tama struts up to the orc corpse and gets ready to take a huge bite—but then...

"Tama, no!"

"Mwn?"

The second Tama's about to take a bite, Aria's shrill voice stops him. She picks him up and hugs him close to her chest.

"Now, if you eat monster meat, you'll get a stomachache! No-no!"

Aria chides Tama.

*Argh...this is bad. If I'm forbidden to eat monsters, I won't be able to acquire new skills moving forward. What to do...?*

There's no way Aria can foresee how Tama feels, as she begins the job of cutting off a piece of the orc.

"Tama, what do you want to do tonight?"

"M-meowww—"

After defeating the orc, today's activities are finished, and Aria and Tama have arrived back at the guild.

Aria's pouch is packed to the brim with goblin ears, and in the hand she's not using to carry Tama, she's holding the orc's arm, stuffed inside a leather bag.

An orc's ears are proof of defeating one—just like goblins—but orc skin and bones fetch a pretty decent price, so Aria brought home a whole arm.

"Good afternoon, Anna. I'm here to declare my quest and have my materials assessed; is that okay?"

"Aria...no time right now. Please go home today."

"Anna…what's the matter?"

Aria steps toward the counter where the receptionist Arnold Holzweilzenegger waits, covered in skintight bondage gear from head to toe as always.

What's going on? Arnold is speaking in a hushed tone—he's definitely being wary of his surroundings.

And just then…

"I've been waiting for you, Aria."

A man appears. He has high-quality equipment but an unspeakably odd face. His hair is chock-full of product and slicked back all the way… It's Kussman.

"Kussman…do you have some business with me?"

"Yes, that's exactly right. Aria, I have some rather unfortunate news for you today."

Even after what happened yesterday, Kussman still thinks he can engage Aria, and she openly shows an air of discomfort. Kussman looks at her lecherously and pushes a letter written on parchment toward her.

"What the—? What is this supposed to be?!"

Seeing the letter, Aria's face is awash with surprise.

The document includes the family seal of Kussman's estate—the Baron Estate—and in summary, the text reads as follows:

Extermination order for the harmful vermin (the elemental cat pet of the adventurer known as Aria) that inflicted bodily harm upon the eldest son of the Baron Estate, Kussman.

*Master?! You look blue in the face… What is this?? An extermination order…for me?!*

Tama now finally understands the situation, having peeked at the letter out of curiosity after seeing the color drain from Aria's face.

Only now does he understand that, in order to protect his master, he has inflicted injury upon a man who happens to be the eldest son of the Baron Estate.

Much the same as other aristocrats, Kussman is prideful. Somehow, in the process of trying to make Aria his very own, bodily harm was inflicted upon his face in a public location, and having endured this mortification, he is angered from his depths. Using his influence as a son of the Baron Estate, he was able to have an extermination order for Tama issued.

"That's simply… No…NO!!"

Tama is so cute and lovely, and he saved her life from certain tragedy. There is no way she will accept this.

However, for commoners, an aristocrat's order is absolute.

Aria begins crying, aware she's hedged in by common law, and squeezes Tama tightly, crouching low to the ground. Her protective stance warns, *If you're going to kill Tama, you'll have to kill me first.*

The surrounding adventurers, witnessing Aria's anguish, exchange words.

"Isn't there something we can do…?"

"No chance. Kussman is the eldest son of the Baron Estate! Not a damn thing doing."

Even the all-powerful receptionist, Arnold, has clenched his eyes shut in pain. Even though he (she?) is *the* Arnold, he's powerless in the face of official aristocratic privilege.

*This is a pickle… What to do? If I find an opening and make a run for it, I'll likely be safe. But that's purely illogical—if I do, I'll be separated from my master. I will be unable to fulfill my oath as a knight to protect her. This is arduous.*

His life in jeopardy—

His knight's oath—

Two options—and Tama is forced between a rock and a hard

place. He conjures a solution in a frenzy while hiding between Aria's breasts.

"Ohhh...poor young Aria. Is this elemental cat *that* important to you?"

Aria denounces Kussman to his face, eyes filled with tears.

Yet Tama has noticed something. Kussman may be putting on a soft, affectionate voice, but his eyes are murky like a river bottom...

"Well then, Aria, what do you think of this? Let's have a duel."

"A...duel? What in the...?"

"Well, it's just that your affection for your pet has really plucked at my heartstrings. I really feel bad for you. Yet, for a man of the Baron Estate to rescind an order he's given is, well, simply not a good look. Hence, the duel. We'll wager the extermination order on the duel, and if you win, I'll rescind it... What do you think?"

Kussman speaks exaggeratedly. But this means that Aria has a chance. Even so, she still looks anguished, and it's obvious why. After all, Aria is D rank, and Kussman is C rank.

Their difference in strength is evident, as is the quality of their equipment. Aria coming out victorious is essentially impossible.

"Don't make that face, Aria. I didn't say we'd be fighting one-on-one."

"...?!"

"From what I hear, you started your adventurer activities with that elemental cat by your side, right? In that case, I'll allow you to face me with him, together."

Aria now looks perplexed at Kussman's loud proclamation.

*If I have Tama with me...*

Hope buds in Aria's heart, yet only for an instant. Her expression soon darkens as she asks Kussman, "What's in this for you?"

Kussman created the extermination order himself, but now he's acting under the pretense of giving Aria a chance. His actions are totally unnatural, and Aria has a hunch that he definitely has another motive.

"Heh-heh-heh…Aria. You are truly intelligent. Yes, exactly as you presumed—there is something in it for me. Let's clarify the terms of this duel. First, if you win, I will rescind the extermination order. That stays the same. What I'd like to add are the conditions upon my victory. Aria…if I win, I will take you as my wife. Those are the terms."

"……!!"

Aria swallows a lump in her throat. Of course, Kussman has an ulterior motive. Well, calling it *ulterior* isn't really right—this was probably his true intention all along.

Kussman has turned the situation in which Aria's pet, Tama, caused him injury, to avoid the roundabout show of getting her to join his party first, cutting to the chase to make her his own.

"Well, what of it, Aria? Will you accept the duel? Or…?"

"I-I'll do it! I accept your duel! So don't even think of trying to kill him here…"

Kussman asks Aria with a lecherous look on his face—truly, he's threatening her—and Aria sobs through tears as she accepts the terms of the duel.

If she refuses, Tama will be dead on the spot—Aria has no other choice but to accept.

*You bastard!*

Anger takes control of Tama's body in a way he has never felt before.

It's directed toward Kussman, who has made his lovely master cry, but above all else, it is self-recrimination for visiting this situation upon both of them.

Tama swears he'll make Kussman pay for the sin of making his master cry.

⊰⊱

"Okay then, Aria. You're sure?"

"Yes, please. Thank you, Anna."

Aria answers Arnold with a quiet nod as adventurers gather around in the rear courtyard of the guild to see how the duel plays out.

"Now shall commence a duel between the C-ranked adventurer of the Baron Estate, Kussman, and the D-ranked adventurer Aria, with her pet, Tama. If the former is victorious, he shall receive the latter as his bride, and her pet will be exterminated. If the latter wins, the extermination order will be rescinded. Does either party object?"

Arnold confirms the terms of the duel after being asked by Aria to see the affair through.

"Of course no."

"I do not."

There's no way Kussman can object—he created this situation. He shakes his head with a coy smile. In comparison, this is the only path Aria has. She defers in consternation.

The duel will be decided by any of the following factors:

- Either party dies.
- Either party signals forfeit.
- The onlookers determine that either party is incapable of battle.

If any of these conditions is met, the victor will be declared.

"Now, both parties at the ready! Begin the duel!"

"Meow!" *Icicle Lance!*

The second Arnold gives the signal, Tama—overcome with rage—attacks immediately. He's chosen the frozen ice spear, Icicle Lance, aiming for the left side of Kussman's chest.

Kussman has sinned by making his master cry... Tama doesn't intend to make him regret it—he intends to kill him with one shot.

But—

"Heh-heh-heh...no chance."

Kussman laughs, fearless, and doesn't even feign a dodge—what does this mean?

In the next instant, a rainbow-colored mist envelops Kussman's body. The Icicle Lance, on course for a direct hit on Kussman, connects with the mist and disappears into thin air.

"What the—?!"

Aria cries out as Tama's attack is rendered null.

"That's my Magic Protection Ring... It's a family heirloom that my adventurer father passed down to me—a magic item that negates magic skills."

Aria and Tama are shocked as Kussman shows off the ring on his right middle finger with pride.

*Shit...so that's what it was. I knew he had something up his sleeve when he agreed to fight me at the same time, but I can't believe he was hiding something like that!*

Tama grits his teeth in annoyance at Kussman's explanation. Because everyone has mistaken Tama for an elemental cat, he can only use elemental magic skills.

Tama has never been a threat to Kussman from the start—that's why he allowed Aria and Tama to fight him two versus one.

"Okay—Aria! Your elemental cat is powerless against me. You might as well surrender now."

"Grrr...Tama, fall back. Acceleration!"

*Surrender, my ass!*

Aria faces Kussman with one thing in mind—to save Tama from extermination.

*Damn, she's fast! But you're too simplistic, Aria.*

Aria rushes toward Kussman with lightning speed, but as a C-ranked adventurer, he can track her with his naked eye. He grips his sword and deflects Aria's knife slash with precision.

"Crap—!!"

Aria backsteps immediately as a kick from Kussman grazes her ribs, causing her perfect white skin to flush red.

"So you managed to evade my kick? That innate skill of yours… Acceleration. The rumors of your speed are true. But that's all you got!"

Finishing his spiel, Kussman leaps forward—it's his turn to attack.

*Not going to allow it!*

In response, Aria reaches down to the garter belt on her thigh and lets two throwing knives fly with a *whoosh*, aiming for Kussman's face.

"Just like I said—too simplistic, Aria!"

Kussman grips the sleeve of his cloak and pulls it up to conceal himself. Aria's throwing knives connect with it but lose all velocity and are easily deflected.

But he's not done yet—Kussman rushes forward and slices down with his sword.

Is he really letting his sword fly without looking in front of himself first? Because she didn't expect this attack, Aria's dodge is a second late.

"Meow!" *No way!*

The instant Kussman's sword is about to connect with Aria's—

Tama flies into the air and rushes directly in between Kussman's blade and her body.

*Shakkin—!!*

The sound of metal on metal erupts through the courtyard.

Kussman's blade has collided with the helmet of Tama's new armor.

*Oof...so heavy...!*

The force of the impact rushes throughout Tama's entire body before he's thrown to the ground in a huff.

"Tama! What are you thinking?!"

Aria raises her voice in a cry of anguish as Tama defends her.

*It should be obvious. I am your knight—it's my job to put my life on the line for you.*

Tama stands up, legs shaking heavily from the pain of being rocked in the head.

"Hmph... This vermin protected Aria from my sword strike. Incredible! Let's see how much you can really stand!"

Kussman begins swinging his blade again, and they're not any normal strikes. He's slashing up and down, left and right, and showing feints—a combination of antipersonnel sword techniques.

"Gah...oof...!"

Aria is fighting to defend each strike. She's only ever fought monsters, and going up against Kussman's swordplay, as a trained aristocrat, has her at a disadvantage. Her two-handed knife defense is quickly broken.

*Crap...!!*

Tama flies in to defend Aria from danger again. Risking his life, he intercepts each lethal strike to save Aria, while she screams through tears, "Tama, no!"

"Heh-heh-heh... What's the matter, vermin? Have you seen enough?"

"M-meowww..."

Kussman ridicules Tama as his defense is nearly broken. Looking closely, he is bleeding from all the places on his body not covered by his armor. Although the cuts aren't deep, Kussman's repeated sword strikes have injured him.

*I won't let you…touch my master! I will protect her!*

Tama again tries to stand, but he cannot. He's bleeding too much to raise himself.

"No… Stop… No more, Tama…!"

Seeing Tama, Aria throws down her knives and drops to her knees to hug and cover him, saying, "I'm sorry, I'm sorry," over and over.

Is she apologizing for getting him into this situation?

Or is she apologizing for being so weak that she requires his constant protection…?

"Well then, Aria, does that mean you forfeit? If you vow to accept me and everything about me, becoming my wife, then I might just be able to spare your elemental cat's life…"

"Are you serious…? You would spare him?!"

"Yes, of course. I'm a man of my word."

Aria's eyes well with tears as she comes to grips with Kussman's proposal. Seeing this, he nods in satisfaction, affirming their bargain.

In reality, he's not interested in taking Tama's life as long as he can have Aria. But putting him on the execution block and then reaching out to save him should allow Aria to become submissive, and thus, his very own.

Everything is going according to his plan.

*Heh-heh-heh…Aria. My oh my, once you become mine, how should we enjoy ourselves? Maybe just in the traditional sense? Or it might be nice to make you hurt and hear that voice…ha!! I can hardly stand it, just imagining…!!*

And that's how it starts—imagining living alongside Aria, Kussman is rife with excitement. His face is twisted in a wicked smile of satisfaction, and all the adventurers waiting on the outcome of the duel are aghast.

*No chance! I cannot allow this brute to take my master. If that happens...*

Tama is equally appalled at the look of madness on Kussman's face. There is no worse fate than having Aria defiled by this man.

"Heh-heh-heh... Well then, admit your defeat. Aria..."

Kussman approaches Aria, still huddled on the ground.

*That's it...*

In the instant Kussman takes his next step, Tama mews quietly.

"Meow—" *Aether Howl!*

*Whoooosh—!!!!*

An explosive rush of wind erupts and blasts Kussman backward. As he had just lifted his leg to step forward, he completely loses his balance and is rocked to the ground with a massive crash.

His arms and legs are splayed in every direction...

"Tama...was that...? Did you...?"

Tama has used a skill that's not magic-based in front of Aria. She might know he's a monster now. But it doesn't matter—as long as she isn't defiled by that absolute cretin.

Tama looks at peace.

"Oy, what just happened?!"

"I dunno! I heard Aria's elemental cat cry out, and then Kussman just went flying!"

"Aria, now's your chance—take him out!"

The surrounding adventurers are in an uproar. The ones especially in love with Aria shout encouragement her way.

Aria is speechless as she puts Tama back on the ground before heading toward Kussman, who's lying immobile from confusion and searing pain.

And then—

"How dare you try to hurt my Tama…"

Aria stares down at Kussman with the iciest of looks and raises her beautiful leg high in the sky.

"W-wait, Aria… You're not going to— Oh my god! No!"

Aria's leg rushes through the air. Realizing where she's aiming, Kussman cries out. He's lying with his legs spread wide and a dislocated hip—he can't close them.

He's obviously incapable of battle, but for *some reason*, Arnold hasn't noticed.

"Heh-heh, it's no use now—with *that thing* hanging between your legs, I can't help but conjure up ideas."

Aria smiles as she shuts down Kussman's plea before adding another line.

"Say good-bye."

Her heel lands, with the final syllable, directly where she was aiming, with a horrendous ripping sound.

"Aria is victorious!"

The female guild staff and female adventurers in the crowd erupt into cries of joy at Arnold's declaration of victory. Conversely, seeing Kussman unconscious with spittle coming from his mouth, every man in the crowd holds his crotch uncomfortably.

"Tama! I'll get you a potion as soon as I can…!"

Aria returns to Tama immediately after dropping Kussman and takes a potion from Arnold, putting it to Tama's lips.

As he's being healed, Tama feels intense relief at having saved his master, before slipping unconscious.

"An innate skill…you say?"

After the duel, Aria is brought to the employee break room at the guild, where she looks puzzled. Tama has been returned to health by the potion and is cuddling in between her breasts.

"Yes. The skill Tama activated at the end was an innate skill, I believe. I've seen an elemental cat with innate skills when I was an adventurer, so I'm quite positive."

Arnold answers Aria, who is relieved that Tama has recovered. The second he did, a concern grew within her—just what was the technique that Tama used at the end of the duel?

Arnold has answered her, saying that it's likely an innate skill.

"It was so powerful, I thought he might be a monster for a second, but I've never heard of a monster that looks like Tama. If he was one, he should also have more mana."

Arnold continues speaking. Normally, the amount of mana flowing from animals and monsters is vastly different, largely thanks to their bodies' physiological differences.

That said, Tama is a monster, but he was a human knight in a past life. He's unconscious of it, but he can regulate and manipulate the mana running through him just like a human being. That means his mana is on the same level as a normal animal.

Arnold is a former B-ranked adventurer and has excellent mana-detection skills. Judging from past experience and the amount of mana flowing out of Tama, he's determined that Tama is not a monster.

*Hmm. In order to protect my master, I was prepared to have*

*my identity as a monster discovered...but it seems that I've been thrown a bone. Not to mention, the fact that elemental cats with innate skills actually exist in our wide world is incredible.*

Reflecting on these developments while also being thankful that his identity is still safe, Tama breathes a sigh of relief. He's also thankful for Arnold's mistake—just like before.

In any case...regarding the root cause of this entire episode— Kussman—it's said that he was completely *broken* by Aria's final heel smash and was unable to be healed through potions... and that according to doctors, his manhood no longer functions.

That said, Kussman has no right to say anything about the matter. A duel is an official battle sanctioned by law. No matter what the results, they must be accepted.

If he tries to plan revenge, the law will come down on him hard—aristocrat or not. For this reason, Aria and Tama will not need to worry about him coming around again.

Kussman played a dirty trick to get Aria to fall into his hand. The fact that he's now incapable of sleeping with a woman ever again smacks deeply of irony.

"Okay, Tama, open wide!"

"Meowrrr—"

Aria is feeding Tama meat from a fork in their room at the inn.

*Wow, this is delicious! I didn't expect anything of the food here, but they're doing it up properly!*

It's still late afternoon, but in order to celebrate today's victory, Aria and Tama are having a toast.

Aria is drinking her favorite fruit liqueur, and Tama has a

special serving of gourmet milk. Their accompaniments include a braised meat dish, grilled fish, and more, prepared by the female proprietor of the inn. They've taken dishes back up to their room, where they're smacking their lips in delight.

Delicious alcohol and tasty food mixed with the lingering aftertaste of victory... Aria and Tama are stuffing themselves.

Just then—

*Hmm? What's the matter, master?*

Tama is chomping down on a piece of grilled fish when he realizes Aria's fork has stopped moving. She has a dark expression, eyes downcast.

"Tama...!!"

"Meowr?"

Tama stares at Aria with worry, and she suddenly scoops him up in her arms.

"Tama...Tama...Tama..."

Aria tightens her grip and repeats his name multiple times, large tears welling up and pouring out of her eyes.

"Thank you so much for protecting me...but please, never do anything that dangerous ever again... If you died, I...I would..."

*Ah...I see what's on your mind.*

Tama infers—Aria is likely remembering what Tama looked like when he was injured protecting her. Now that she's consumed alcohol, her emotions have exploded.

*Don't worry, my master... I have no intention of perishing so easily. And now, if something happens, I can use my Elemental Howl. I also plan on using Iron Body, as necessary, so what happened this time will never repeat itself.*

The commotion of the duel has left Tama unhindered. The Aether Howl he used in the nick of time in the final moment has been confused as an innate skill. He intends to bring out his other skills as necessary in any dangerous situation he approaches moving forward.

"Meowrrr—"

Tama mews tenderly, brushing his face against Aria's cheek to wipe away her tears.

"Aw…you're the one who got hurt, but you're still cheering me up… You are such a sweetheart, Tama."

Aria finally smiles again, impressed by Tama's consideration toward her. He continues comforting her long into the night.

"Hmm, which one should I choose…?"

The day after the duel, in midafternoon—Aria puts her index finger to her lips, perplexed. She's at Vulcan's item shop, in the dagger and knife corner.

Kussman's fierce attacks during yesterday's duel put huge chips in both her knives, dulling them. She's determined that they cannot be repaired and has decided to buy brand-new ones. It's already midafternoon because of the expected hangover and because Vulcan, the owner of the shop, is often delving into the labyrinth in the morning anyway.

Speaking of Vulcan…

"Meow! Tama is as calm and cute as ever!"

Vulcan, dressed in her quintessential bare-skinned overall look, takes Tama from Aria and places him in between her exposed breasts. She's taken quite the shine to the cute little elemental cat, and it shows in her loving expression.

"Meowr—"

Tama closes his eyes in bliss and wavers on the line of

consciousness. Tama is a knight on the inside but still looks like a behemoth cub. He's tired from yesterday, and his eyes are drooping.

"Oh, this looks like a good one."

Aria has finally found a knife she's interested in among the large selection. She takes it in her hand and slashes with it a few times. The knife rips through the air, and Aria feels like it's easier to wield than her old knives, with excellent responsiveness.

"This is a fine blade...and the price... Oof..."

Aria looks miffed. Proper quality weapons definitely come with a price.

Yesterday—during her quest before the duel—Aria was able to take home goblin ears and the orc arm, and she has some extra money. But if she buys two of the knives she's holding in her hand, she'll use nearly all her earnings.

Thinking about the money it will cost for maintenance on the blades, she can't help but hesitate.

"Meow, Aria? Sorry to bother you while you're selecting weapons, but I have something I'd like to ask you. It's not anything that will bother you, I don't think."

"What is it? It's rare of you to come to me for advice."

Aria often seeks Vulcan's counsel regarding weapons, but Vulcan asking Aria, her customer, for advice is quite rare. Aria looks puzzled while she wonders what it could be.

"Actually, the thing is, I'm currently looking for adventurers to partner up with. If it's okay with you, won't you form a party together?"

"Wow...? Really, Vulcan, a party with you and me?"

"Yes, meow! I feel sheepish saying it, but because I'm C rank, you joining me could be a good thing, right?!"

"I am flattered...but why me, of all people? I'm only D rank, and, Vulcan, you had the ex-knight commanding officer Sakura in your party before, right…?"

Aria looks elated at Vulcan's invite—she, too, has been wanting to partner up with female adventurers. The main reasons she's been taking on solo quests so far are her dislike of men and the fact that few reasonable female adventurers exist around here.

Now that Vulcan, who always treats her well—and is of higher rank—has asked her to join up together, she definitely has a reason to be excited.

At the same time, she also has her doubts. Just as she said to Vulcan, she's only recently graduated from the beginner stages and is still merely a D rank. And Vulcan had a B-ranked adventurer named Sakura as her partner in the past.

"Rank is not an issue. I've been hearing about your potential, and after yesterday's duel, all the adventurers are talking about how strong Tama is. Also…"

"Also…?"

Vulcan offers high praise for Aria and Tama but suddenly looks disheartened and hesitates to continue, prompting Aria to ask her what's up.

"Also…Sakura and I broke up our party yesterday. Actually, it turns out she conceived a 'magic-wielding girlie-boy from another world.'"

"Ohhh…is that so…?"

Aria senses that something is off from the words *another world* and *girlie-boy*, but she accepts the situation. It's not rare for people from another world to visit this one, and adventurer parties disbanding due to a member becoming pregnant is also common.

…In reality, the magic-wielding feminine boy and Sakura are both connected to the Sword Saint Aria longs to meet…but that is a story for another time.

"That's the gist of it, so whaddaya say? Will you form a party with me? If you do now, I can offer you equipment at special party rates!"

"If that's the case, I have no reason to say no! Tama—you think it's a good idea, too, right?"

"Meow!"

Aria responds positively as Vulcan presses her again, and Tama concurs with a hearty mew.

*It's a great thing for my master to have a partner. It only reduces her risk of being slain, and what's more—Vulcan already owns her own shop. She's completely trustworthy.*

Tama has no objection to forming a party with Vulcan.

"Okay, then! We'll commence activities tomorrow morning. We'll meet at the guild, okay meow?"

"Of course, no problem. Hee-hee, I can't wait, Vulcan."

"Me too! Meow!"

Aria and Vulcan shake heartily on their new partnership.

Porcelain-white skin on a female elf beauty and wheat-colored skin on a tiger-eared babe. Joining them is a behemoth who's been mistaken as an elemental cat.

Labyrinthos has a unique new party in town.

*Ga-gan—!!*

A goblin is rocked by a blunt-force attack and blasted far across the room. The girl left standing has amber skin and overalls, short golden hair, and cat ears... It's Vulcan.

Yet there are a few things different about her today. She has rough gauntlets on both her hands and similar leggings wrapped around both legs. And she grips a large hammer the same size as herself—a battle hammer—in her gauntlets.

The goblin faced her battle hammer's wrath and was blasted across the room.

*"Gi-gii—"*

*And your comrade, too!*

Showing bitter resentment, another goblin grips its dagger and flies at Vulcan.

Goblins are imbeciles. The second they see a human, they come rushing at them—no matter who it is. That means no matter how strong their adversary...

"Just what the hell does a goblin have to do with me?!"

They're really such a pain, goblins. Vulcan lifts her battle hammer with ease, truly unimaginable given her delicate figure, and brings it down on the goblin before it can reach her.

*Splat—*

The monster eats a heavy blow straight to the cranium and is turned into a literal pancake. Blood and viscera fly through the air. For an adventurer, this sight is a daily occurrence.

"Absolutely incredible. Vulcan! You are a true member of the tiger-eared clan!"

As Vulcan wipes the blood from her battle hammer, Aria addresses her from the rear guard. Tama is pawing around near her feet.

It's morning in the upper layers of the labyrinth. Just as promised last night, Aria and Vulcan have joined forces on their first quest.

"Come on meow, I eat goblins for breakfast!"

Vulcan raps her battle hammer on her shoulder as she responds to Aria's praise. It's true that Vulcan looks cool and relaxed, nowhere close to short of breath. The way she wields a heavy weapon like a battle hammer so lightheartedly should be completely impossible.

*Wow, I knew Vulcan was part of the tiger-eared clan, but I definitely didn't think she had this level of superhuman strength.*

Tama is also glued to Vulcan's display of prowess. The secret to her unnatural level of strength lies in her race—the tiger-eared clan.

As stated previously, the tiger-eared clan is a race of demihumans. They have tiger blood running in them, and although they look slender, their muscular composition is completely different from the average human.

If asked how strong, they can easily carry an entire midsize monster on their backs all the way out of the labyrinth. That is the reason Vulcan can delve into the labyrinth on her own and return with a large amount of raw materials.

Vulcan is also currently shouldering a big leather backpack. Today's quest involves defeating one minotaur, which Tama has also defeated previously. They're C-ranked monsters...

Tama was worried it might be too early for a minotaur for Aria, but after receiving certification from the receptionist lady (?) Arnold that she'll be fine with Vulcan along, he's now at ease.

"Okay, let's get their ears off before moving onward!"

"Yep!"

With Vulcan's superhuman strength and her backpack, they could easily bring back an entire goblin corpse, but they won't.

The minotaur they're after won't appear until the fifth level or below. Carrying something so heavy all the way down would be inane. Also, after defeating the minotaur, they'll dissect it to bring the whole corpse with them, while also picking up different ores and minerals for blacksmithing on their way out.

The second layer of the labyrinth—

*"Gi-gya—!"*
*"Gugi-gya-gya—!"*
Another horde of goblins appears in tandem with their screeching voices. Four total... Judging from their number, Aria could likely take them down herself, but the labyrinth is a fickle beast.

*"Gu-giii!"* Fireball!
One of the goblin group casts the low-level fire elemental spell Fireball. It's a goblin mage—the same type that put Aria between a rock and a hard place previously.

The fireball surges forward, but Tama and Aria remain motionless because Vulcan has commanded them to watch. It's easier for them to watch than for her to explain. Vulcan intends to show them how she fights solo so they completely understand her capabilities.

"Just who do you think you are meow?!"
As she speaks, Vulcan swings her battle hammer from the side. She connects directly with the fireball, and it erupts in a massive roar and creates a small explosion.

"Meow it's my turn!"
Vulcan flies out from behind the blast. The goblin's eyes are bugging out of its head from the sudden turn of events. But just what is happening? Vulcan's battle hammer isn't in her hands.

"Enchant Flame!"
Vulcan utters these words as she rushes forward. Suddenly, both her gauntlets are engulfed in flame.

*Bwohhh—!*
Vulcan throws a fist that rips a blaze through the air. Her punch

lands directly in the goblin's gut with a *thud*, followed by a hot sizzle of flesh.

"*Ga-gyahhh!!*"

Its stomach burned to a crisp, the goblin mage loses consciousness and tumbles to the ground. Vulcan brings her steel leggings down on the goblin's head and crushes its skull.

It's far from over—many enemies remain.

Now Vulcan turns all five fingers and aligns them vertically, aiming for the next goblin's stomach with a fierce thrust. The blade of her hand—wrapped in flame—pierces the goblin's stomach and sears it from the inside.

There's definitely no chance of coming back from that one. Blood and smoke gush from the goblin's mouth as it crumples in a heap. As far as the remaining two goblins...their fate goes without saying.

As Vulcan takes the life of the last of them, Aria asks, "Vulcan, what was that skill...?"

"That was a derived skill that grants elemental powers extrapolated from my blacksmithing capabilities, called 'Enchant.' It allows me to put elemental effects on different items!"

"I see, a 'derived skill,' huh?"

The types of skills that humans possess are generally limited to the two types previously discussed—innate skills possessed since birth and skills acquired from magic items called scrolls.

However, there are exceptions. They include the type Vulcan just mentioned, the derived skill Enchant. Derived skills refer to evolved skills developed from capabilities that the user refines over a long period, allowing them to optimize that functionality within their own personal characteristics. In Vulcan's case, her aptitude for blacksmithing has evolved and turned into a battle skill.

*I see. Vulcan uses her tiger-eared-clan superhuman strength to*

*wield the battle hammer and her derived skill Enchant to bash her*
*enemies, even empty-handed... I see what makes her a C-ranked*
*adventurer now.*

After seeing Vulcan's battle prowess, Tama is totally convinced that Arnold giving the *go* sign for this quest was a spot-on judgment.

Just then—

"*Snort*—"

A swine-faced orc appears, squealing like a pig.

"Vulcan, I understand your true capability now. This round, please observe our power, too. Let's go, Tama!"

"Meow!"

Aria reins in Vulcan, who's gripping her battle hammer, and steps forward. Tama is also ready to wreck. Having seen Vulcan throwing down, his battle spirit is on fire.

"Acceleration!"

Aria rushes forward with blinding speed. She has to show the girl who invited her into her party, Vulcan, that she has what it takes. No matter what—

"What did you think, Vulcan?"

Aria wipes the sweat from her brow. The corpse of the orc lies at her feet...with a knife buried deeply in its eye. Just like before, she used Tama's support from the rear, and when the orc recoiled, she took advantage of the opening and laced a knife straight into the orc's cranium.

"What tremendous speed. Your innate skill, Acceleration... I'd heard the rumors, but I didn't think it would be like that! And Tama's cover was sheer purrfection!"

Impressed at seeing Aria's speed, Vulcan offers words of sincere admiration. Complimented by an adventurer of higher rank, Aria looks elated.

However…

Vulcan suddenly looks serious and says, "Yet there are definitely a few things you need to learn in terms of fighting style."

"Things to learn?"

"That's right, meow. Your attacks are superfast, but your movements are all in direct lines and very simplistic. Going up against goblins and orcs isn't an issue, but monsters with intellectual capacity like minotaurs will be another issue."

*I see—Vulcan has ascertained Aria's weakness, too.*

Tama is impressed at what Vulcan has said and thanks god she pointed it out to Aria.

Because Aria has the superior innate skill Acceleration, she has the tendency to utilize its capacity and move as fast as possible when attacking as well. Of course, moving quickly is a great thing, but her move set doesn't include any feints aside from when she uses her throwing knives.

What's more, calling the action she employs when she uses a throwing knife a feint is a bit naive. These are a few of the reasons Aria didn't stand a chance in her duel against Kussman the other day.

*Because I can't speak, even though I can assist my master, I cannot offer her advice. But Vulcan, on the other hand…*

This is the true definition of *Thank god.*

"I've got it! We've started a party together, and we should definitely use this as a chance to train you!"

"Are you serious? Please, that would be amazing. I want to get stronger!"

Aria answers Vulcan with enthusiasm.

In the past—ever since the Sword Saint saved her—Aria has

always wanted to get stronger, and one could say that reaction is natural.

*Meowr—I think we really found a winner with Vulcan. We haven't met anyone this committed to self-improvement, ever!*

Seeing Aria's stance, Vulcan is deeply impressed. With Aria, she might be able to reach the same level as she did with Sakura—no, she might even be able to eclipse her.

Vulcan's lips curl into a smile as she says, "In that case, there's a *perfect* monster for you waiting on the next level!"

Seeing Vulcan's face, for some reason, Aria is gripped with a frightening chill.

*Squelch, squelch, shpleeem—*

Having stepped foot into the third level of the labyrinth, Aria and company are confronted with two writhing figures.

"Oof… Vulcan, when you said *'perfect'* monster, you couldn't have possibly been talking about *that*, could you?!"

"Heh-heh, you're spot-on. No matter how much you hate it, going up against these things, you won't be able to use direct-line movement. You'll be in a world of hurt if one catches you."

Looking at the wriggling monstrosities, Aria is slack-jawed throughout Vulcan's response.

Writhing figures—

Captivating green bodies covered in tentacles…and slick with a squelching, thick mucus dripping off them.

These monsters are called "ropers."

On Earth, these plant-based monsters appear in games and comic books, walking definitions of the word *aberration* that portend they will not tolerate anything following them. They don't have any real attack power, but anyone caught by them just once will be in a world of misery. They cover their captives' entire bodies in mucus and use their tentacles on every last part of the human body... Let's stop there.

*Can I really let my master...an angel...an elf...her melons...? Can I really let her go up against these things alone?! Vulcan—just what morbid pretext are you acting under?!*

Tama shudders with fear at Vulcan's proposal.

"Okay, Aria. This is another part of your training! Escape the grasp of those writhing tentacles and defeat it for us! Of course, Tama can't help you."

"Uuugh...okay, I got it! Accelerate!"

Aria's skin is rippling with goose bumps just thinking about what would happen if she were to get caught as she activates her specialty, Acceleration, and approaches the two ropers.

*Shloop—*

One of the pair stretches its tentacles at Aria as she rushes toward them. Its movements were slow and meandering earlier, but the tentacles now move at unbelievable speed.

In contrast with their appearance, ropers have excellent dynamic vision, and their tentacles are lightning quick.

*I see—this will be excellent training after all.*

Aria thinks this as she circles wide to avoid the outstretched tentacles. In the same moment, realizing she won't be able to avoid two of the tentacles, she grips her knife in the opposite hand and slices through them with a snap.

"*Pi-gyah—?!*"

The roper cries out in anguish at its tentacle being slashed off. However, now it's spinning all its appendages out in a radial pattern and rushing toward Aria.

"Damn—"

Aria is appalled as she cries out—even if she cuts off some of the tentacles, she's still at risk of being caught by the others. Not to mention, another roper waits silently close by, biding its time for the perfect moment to expose Aria's blind spot and attack.

Aria sprints away—but this time, it's not a direct line like before. She rushes in an ebb and flow of movement with sudden changes in tempo. She throws feints, stepping quickly left and right. Her movements have matured, largely dependent on her singular desire to not be snared.

"Now!"

"*Piiiii—?!*"

Aria has predicted exactly where the roper's tentacle would recede and create an opening as she rushes in close. Then she screams with abandon and does a midair cartwheel, taking her knives in both hands and shredding every one of the roper's arms off at the base.

"Now the next one! Oh—no, god!!"

Aria realizes that if she steps in to finish off the first roper, she will be immediately wrapped up by the second. She decides to kick the first roper, now void of tentacles, back with all her might.

But that was a bad decision.

The second she kicks the roper back, milk-white mucilage sprays from every one of its severed tentacle holes, due to the pressure, and lands directly on Aria's face.

"Daaamn…she messed up now. And that visual is absolutely nasty."

"Meow!!" *My master!!*

Aria is sweating from the battle, her face flushed red, and breathing rough. In this condition, with that sort of white all over her face, it's simply…wrong.

Vulcan is clasping her hands together in deep regret, while

Tama cries out in anguish at the sight of his master reduced to this level of "pseudo-bukkake."

"Ugh...I can't believe this!! I would only allow Tama to do this to me!!"

Aria is pissed. Her fetish definitely doesn't extend to all inter-species relations. She loves cats, and she's deeply in love with the adorable Tama, who saved her life. She's already committed in her heart of hearts to losing her virginity to him.

But now, this disgusting monster has defiled her face... She cannot forgive this.

Aria kicks the roper waiting next to her. More mucilage rains down on her, but what does she care at this point?

The roper is rocked backward. Aria chases it down...but then she actually rushes right past it.

"Meowr?! Aria, what are you doing—?!"

"Meow!" *What's the matter, master?*

Both Vulcan and Tama cry out in surprise. But then—in that second, *it* happens.

*Slash—rip—ppplsssh—*

Blasted backward, the roper's tentacles are being sheared off one by one. By the time it's plastered against the back wall, every last one of them is lying on the ground.

Vulcan and Tama have no idea what they just witnessed. Aria whispers to herself.

"I just learned 'Whirlwind Slash.'"

""Meowr?!""

Aria said Whirlwind Slash—the name of a new skill she's learned. It's a derived skill. The fact that Aria was completely help-less in her duel against Kussman and caused Tama to get injured is reality. During her current quest, Vulcan gave her instructions, and she knew she had to make a change.

Acceleration is Aria's innate skill that she's used for many years. But different skills can be derived depending on the user's environment.

Aria wants to get stronger. She never wants to hurt Tama again.

Her hope, love, and anger—together, they caused her Acceleration skill to evolve. As a result, the skill's effect creates a whirlwind of attacks that hit all around her.

As the slashes flew from her body in every direction, the roper got closer and ended up sliced to bits. Now that she moves with tempo and rhythm, she can't let loose the same number of attacks she did when she moved in direct lines.

However, with Whirlwind Slash, she can attack while she's on the move. Because she thrives off speed, it's an ideal skill to have.

"Meowr, come to think of it, when I realized my first derived skill, I also exploded with joy…"

Seeing Aria suddenly realize her first derived skill, Vulcan recalls her own past. Derived skills are often realized in moments least expected…

"Damn—you bastard—!"

In the back of the room, Aria is stabbing the lifeless, disarmed roper repeatedly.

Amen!

*Hmm? This might be a good chance!*

Watching Aria turn the roper's body into a cold-blooded murder scene out of one eye, Tama realizes something. The monster she's stabbing relentlessly is the first of the two—the one that sprayed mucilage onto her face. That means no one's paying attention to the other one. Tama slowly tiptoes over toward the roper by himself, and checking that Aria's not looking…

*Chomp—!*

Tama takes a bite.

*Oof. This tastes terrible. It's bitter and super slimy—downright nasty. But what skill will it give...?*

---

**Name: Tama**
**Type: Behemoth (cub)**
**Innate Skills: Elemental Howl, Skill Absorb,**
**    Elemental Tail Blade**
**Absorbed Skills: Storage, Poison Fang, Flight,**
**    Fireball, Icicle Lance, Iron Body, Summon**
**    Tentacle, Endless Mucus Blast, Crossbreed**

---

*Oh...*

Tama is blown away by the new skills he's obtained. Summon Tentacle, Endless Mucus Blast, and Crossbreed... Just what sort of skills did he acquire?

*Hmm...I guess thinking about it, it's obvious. This was certainly my mistake. Next time, I'll think carefully before eating any monsters. But...Crossbreed, huh? I've heard that ropers can also conceive with human females, but I never thought it would be possible due to a skill...hmm? Wait...cross...breed?*

Repeating the name of the skill to himself, a phrase pops into his head.

*"...Then we'll go meow, meow a lot together, okay?"*

That's right—it's what Aria said to Tama when she initially mistook him for an elemental cat in the guild.

*Shiver—*

This means that Aria's desire could possibly someday become reality. A chill runs down Tama's spine just thinking about it.

"Come now, Aria. I think you've had your fun; it's time to go."

"*Huff...huff...* I'm sorry, Vulcan. I'm coming."

Vulcan addresses Aria while continuing to stab rampantly. A piece of tentacle sticks out from Vulcan's backpack—she's collected it as proof of victory.

"Hmm? Tama? You don't look so well..."

"Mraw...meowrrr...?"

Aria looks at Tama quizzically, but all he can do is maintain his stony face and turn his head to the side, as if saying, *Whatever do you mean?*

The fifth layer of the labyrinth—

"Ugh...my whole body feels wet and slippery..."

"Meowr...it's because you fought that many of them—nothing you can do."

Aria's and Vulcan's faces are both flushed red as their expressions contort. Their faces and heads are covered in slime, as well as everything below the neck.

Just when they thought they'd made it out of the third level, the fourth level was also packed to the brim with ropers. Both knife-wielding Aria and battle hammer–hefting Vulcan used attacks that sent buckets of mucus flying everywhere.

Since they're both close-quarters-combat specialists, it's no surprise they look like this after engaging in a melee battle with ropers.

Since he was devoted to supporting them from the rear guard, Tama has been spared. That said, aside from the fact that their entire bodies are covered in slime, the end result is a positive one—neither of the girls was caught in the ropers' tentacles even once. If they had been, they'd be acting as a roper's seed mother about now.

"Aria. We need to focus."

"You're right. This is the fifth level—a minotaur could appear at any time. Tama, if we need you to, can you use the skill you activated before?"

"Meow!" *Of course, master!*

Even though they've been given Arnold's seal of approval, the minotaur is a C+-ranked monster. According to simple rank, it's far above even Vulcan. For the sake of training, they've been holding Tama back from unleashing his power, but they won't continue doing so forever.

Just a few minutes after exploring the fifth level—

*"Mwohhh—!!"*

Suddenly, a minotaur appears. This one is different from the one Tama previously faced—it has a steel club and shield.

"Aria. It hasn't noticed our presence yet. I need you for a preemptive attack."

"Leave it to me. I'll dive in first with a Whirlwind Slash."

Aria and Vulcan are whispering quietly in the shadow of a rock outcropping.

Aria activates Acceleration and rushes out in a burst.

*"Mwo—?!"*

The minotaur is shocked by Aria's speed and lets out a startled grunt. It immediately reaches for its club, but it's far too late—Aria has already sprinted past it on the side.

*Slash—!* A bloody cut from Aria's Whirlwind Slash runs along the minotaur's front leg.

But…Aria is crestfallen.

"Agh, it's not deep at all."

Just as she said, the cut on the minotaur is quite shallow—it's barely bleeding.

*Hmm... Whirlwind Slash... It's a quick attack, but it doesn't seem very powerful. Ropers and other monsters that are soft should be no problem, but the minotaur is a different story.*

Tama realizes this as he trots behind Aria to protect her.

Minotaurs are covered in a thick armor of muscle. Aria's Whirlwind Slash isn't strong enough to make any severe wounds—

"How about this, then?!"

Vulcan jumps out and raises her battle hammer high, rushing in a direct line toward the minotaur as she swings it down.

The minotaur meets the blow with the shield in its left hand.

Vulcan screams out Aria's name as she watches the minotaur's shield block her blow and takes a backstep to create distance.

"Aria!"

"Okay! If once didn't work, I'll just keep it up, over and over!"

Aria and Vulcan have heightened their cooperative awareness over the third and fourth layers of the labyrinth, and Aria knew what Vulcan was going to say without her even saying it.

She activates Acceleration and Whirlwind Slash again. She approaches the minotaur from the back with a flurry of attacks exploding in all directions.

"Again—attack one!"

Aria's knives cut into the minotaur's back. It's still shallow, but it's causing damage.

The minotaur does a 180-degree turn and raises its club high to smash down Aria.

"Too slow—attack two!"

Aria has activated Acceleration—there's no way she'll get caught by the attack.

By the time its club has whooshed down, Aria has already ducked under its flank, and as she passes by, she lets loose more slash attacks.

Three, four, five—!!

Every time Aria gets close to the minotaur, its body becomes bloodier and bloodier. In turn, its movements are dulled. It's quickly losing blood.

Even though Aria's individual attacks aren't cutting deep, this many slashes definitely takes a toll on the opponent.

*"Mwohhh—!!"*

The minotaur explodes in a cry of rage.

In that second, it discards its club and shield, rushing toward Aria with outstretched arms—it intends to strangle Aria to death. This attack is a complete sacrificial maneuver.

It has likely sensed imminent death due to high blood loss and is hoping to take someone else down with it.

"Tama, help me out!"

"Meow!" *You got it, master!*

Aria is unshaken as she calls out for Tama to follow her. Tama answers with a cute mew before popping out in front of her. And then—

"Meow!" *Aether Howl!!*

Tama activates Aether Howl, one of his Elemental Howls.

The minotaur bearing down on Aria is thrown forcefully backward. Just as with Kussman, the minotaur smashes every last part of its body against the rock floor. It's so shocked from the sudden turn of events, overcome with confusion and pain, that it doesn't make a sound.

"Meow! Leave the rest up to me-ow!"

Sensing her chance, Vulcan leaps into the fray.

She's not as quick as Aria, but the tiger-eared-clan girl Vulcan is also super speedy. She closes the distance to the minotaur in an instant. As it tries to get up, she raises her battle hammer high in the air and crushes its skull.

*Do-gan—!!*

The minotaur's massive body again lies facedown on the rocky earth.

"We did it! This completes our quest!"

"Meowrn?"

Aria cries out with joy and scoops up Tama, elated, sending him directly into a dive between her melons.

Tama is surprised for a second but quickly relaxes and rubs his face into Aria's bosom to praise her.

"Meow—you two are so purrfect together!"

Vulcan laughs sarcastically as Aria and Tama are enraptured with each other's touch.

"Meowr? Another roper, is it…?"

"Oof… Another one, eh…?"

After defeating the minotaur and turning to head back home, Aria and company are confronted by another roper. Remembering how covered in slime she got earlier, Aria scowls.

"Leave this one up to me-ow."

Vulcan leaves Aria aside and approaches the roper for a fight with a cool expression on her face. She's different than Aria—she's laid waste to umpteen ropers in her day, and she's more than used to getting covered in their slime. Not to mention, Aria looks quite tired by now, and she decides to do her a favor and take this one for the team.

"Okay, here we go meow!"

Vulcan cries out and raises her battle hammer before rushing forward. The roper squeals "Pi-giii—!" in response and extends its tentacles toward her in attack.

*Hmm…that voice…!*

Tama can't help but feel something is off about the roper's voice. It's lower in tone than usual and sounds muffled. Hearing it, he remembers the existence of a different monster and rushes in front of Vulcan.

*Ga-kinn—!*

The sharp sound of metal on metal reverberates throughout the room—Tama's helmet against a blade extended from one of the roper's tentacles.

"Meowr?!"

Vulcan's eyes are wide as saucers seeing Tama jump out in front of her to intercept the roper's tentacle blade.

This was no simple roper. It has a special name: blade roper. It's a high-level roper that mutated out of the blue. Aside from its slightly different voice, there is no further information distinguishing it from the regular breed, and the chances of mutation are extremely rare at one in over ten thousand. The world at large has no inkling of their existence.

However, Tama is a battle-tested knight and has faced off against blade ropers in the past. He still remembers its odd cry from that time and, sensing imminent danger, shielded Vulcan from its blade.

*Laying a hand on my master's party member is punishable by death! Eat this! Icicle Lance!*

Although Tama loses his balance from being hit in midair, he composes his inherent behemoth dexterity and bores a hateful gaze into the blade roper. After charging his Icicle Lance for a few seconds, he lets it rip.

"Pi-gyahhhh—!!"

The blade roper's cries of agony reverberate throughout the labyrinth. Pierced by the Icicle Lance, it crumples to the ground.

"Tama! Very good boy! Vulcan, are you okay?"

Tama's quick decision saved Vulcan from a certain dilemma, and Aria praises him as she rushes to Vulcan's side. She can say only one thing...

"Meowr...you definitely just saved my life. What a good, tough boi."

Mumbling to herself, Vulcan stares off in the distance behind Tama.

At a glance, her cheeks have turned a rosy pink, but what of it...?

"Hey, now—!! Vulcan and Aria, welcome back!"

Arnold addresses Aria and company as they return to the guild. He shoots a wink their way, and Tama can't help but nearly turn nauseated at the foul sight of it.

"Anna, sorry to cut to the chase, but we'd like an evaluation right away meow. Oof—!"

Vulcan sloughs the weighty backpack off her shoulders and begins lining up its contents on the counter. An arm and a leg... pieces of the minotaur, which was dismembered and drained of blood. She also pulls out a handful of roper tentacles and goblin ears.

The minotaur's horns and claws have been removed—Vulcan will use them to modify different items.

"Wow, this damage... It can't be from one of your attacks, can it, Vulcan?"

"Meow—nope. Those are cuts from Aria's new skill. She obtained a new derived skill on this quest!"

"Oh, wow, a derived skill?! That's impressive—nice work, Aria!"

Arnold winks again after hearing the news. Aria answers him with a huge grin.

"Okay, I'll put this through for evaluation, so go kill some time as usual, okay?"

"You got it! Aria, do you have any plans in mind later on?"

"No, not really. If you forced me to tell you, I'd say fooling around with—erm, going shopping for dinner with Tama—that's about it."

*Oh god… Just more evidence that rumor is true…*

As Aria stumbles over her words, Vulcan remembers a piece of gossip she heard about her recently. A rumor that explicitly states her fetish is…you know.

But even if it is true, Vulcan has absolutely zero intention of denouncing Aria. For one, she's a demi-human with feline blood running in her ancestry, and though it might be rare in this world, there are certainly beings that beget offspring as a result of relations with animals capable of crossbreeding.

*But thinking about it, the way I'm beginning to perceive Aria's feelings… No, let's forget it for now.*

"In that case, won't you come to the guild bar and have a toast to our new party? My shop is closed today, so I'm totally free right meow."

"Ooh, that's a great idea!"

Hearing Vulcan's suggestion, Aria's elf ears bounce up and down excitedly.

Aria loves the food at the guild bar, and if she's with someone else, she won't have to put up with being hit on while she eats… At least, she doesn't think so, and she's elated at the prospect.

"Okay meow! Let's go!"

"Mmm—!! The food here is so damn good!"

"Meow! I can't believe this is the guild's food!"

Aria and Vulcan swoon as a variety of dishes arrives from the guild kitchen. Tama is also busily chomping away at Aria's side, totally oblivious to his surroundings.

The guild menu is mostly seafood. Labyrinthos has waterways running throughout its entire expanse, and the ocean is close by. For this reason, dinner tables are often found full of the bounty of the sea.

Whitefish carpaccio, bouillabaisse with many different fish and seafood, shellfish pasta... Everything is outstandingly delicious. Among all the dishes, Aria and company's favorite is easily the Hoballe prawn, cooked in the shell.

The Hoballe prawn is a local specialty from this area. At full size, they grow to be as large as an adult human arm and are essentially close to lobsters that exist in the human realm. The main difference is that they are blue and have a slightly sharper edge to their shape. Their flavor is beyond rich, with a unique sweetness, and each bite has wonderful texture. Here at the guild bar, the Hoballe prawn is sliced in half lengthwise and served grilled. It comes with butter sauce, chili sauce, and garlic sauce, making for many ways to enjoy this dish.

Off the subject—but when the dish was first served, the way Aria looked between the butter sauce and Tama with ragged breath was... Well, she just decided to assume that neither Tama nor Vulcan noticed.

*Nonetheless...this is a resplendent sight indeed.*

Aria pushes her fork toward Tama, saying, "Open wide!" as he reflects on the situation.

The utterly fresh and clean, drop-dead-gorgeous elf girl Aria.

The lively and vigorous beast-eared beauty Vulcan.

Tama has thought so previously, but the sight of these two getting along like two peas in a pod is a work of art in itself. To boot, today they've both imbibed alcohol, and their cheeks are flushed—doubly cuter than normal.

The catcalls that usually bother Aria are nowhere to be heard today. The fact that Vulcan is there drinking with her is part of the equation, but seeing the expressions of the men who do come close, she realizes that Tama is threatening them from under the table.

After the duel with Kussman the other day, Tama's latent powers have become quite the rumor. "Beware thee daring to come near the all-powerful Fearsome Cat," they say...

"Meowr—I feel so good right meow! I'm having another."

"Hee-hee—then I definitely am, too!"

Vulcan and Aria both order another round.

*It seems that tonight could be a long one...*

Tama chuckles sarcastically to himself as Aria orders the round and lovingly rubs his head.

The next morning—

*Mmph...I'm up to my neck here.*

Tama is facing a certain conundrum. Moving to the left or moving to the right—*squish*. He is squashed together by a soft embrace on both sides and can't move at all.

Aria is on his right. Every time he moves, she says, "Mmm...oh, Tama, no, that's too rough..." in her sleep...

"Meowr...I might be interested in this fetish, too... Just a little bit..."

On his left, Vulcan is also talking in her sleep.

In other words, Tama is sandwiched between both their breasts. They're on the second floor of Vulcan's item shop—in her bedroom.

Just how did everyone end up in this situation...?

Last night, Aria and Vulcan started getting rowdy and eventually found themselves at Vulcan's place for an after-party. They both got wasted and collapsed on the bed together.

Aria grabbed Tama and forced him in between her melons. Vulcan, who was equally drunk, said, "Let me-ow join the fun, too!" and grabbed onto Aria as they both passed out…and now it's morning. Quite the tale, isn't it?

Come to think of it…Vulcan saying, *"I might be interested in this fetish, too,"* in her sleep… Does that mean…? Well, that's for another time.

*Oh well, my master and Vulcan both battled hard yesterday; they must have been tired. I can't bring myself to wake them. That said, I'm getting totally bored here… Maybe I should double-check my status— Wait, what the hell is this?*

Tama pulls up his status display to kill some time and is in complete shock from one of the items in the list.

---

**Name: Tama**
**Type: Behemoth (cub)**
**Innate Skills: Elemental Howl, Skill Absorb,**
 **Elemental Tail Blade**
**Absorbed Skills: Storage, Poison Fang, Flight,**
 **Fireball, Icicle Lance, Iron Body, Summon**
 **Tentacle, Endless Mucus Blast, Crossbreed**
**Evolution Possible: Behemoth (second form)**

---

*Evolution…?! So that's what this means!*

Tama understands what's happening as he sees the words *Evolution Possible.*

As behemoths are understood in this world, cubs do not reach a new form through the growth of their body but rather through evolution.

*This is part of the reason there is little information on behemoth cubs and no information related to witnessing a behemoth during a growth spurt. If evolution is now possible for me, I must have reached the upper limit of my powers yesterday—in other words, my level—during our battle... At least, that's my assumption.*

Monsters also gain strength from repeated battle experience, just like humans. Yet, unlike humans, when their level increases to a certain extent, they evolve according to the experience gained.

Tama had already attained a certain level of fighting ability as a knight during his past life. In addition, he experienced more than a few fierce battles in the labyrinth soon after he was reborn. Then there was the duel with Kussman, as well as his battles alongside Aria and Vulcan in the labyrinth yesterday.

It has been a very short period of time, but Tama has already participated in a vast number of altercations—far more than any normal monster—which has accordingly increased his level.

*Hmm. This is quite fortunate for me. If I were to gradually grow into a form representative of what people expect from a behemoth, I would not be able to continue protecting my master as her knight. Yet, if I can choose whether or not I want to evolve...*

As long as Tama doesn't choose to evolve, he can stay with Aria forever—and Tama is extremely relieved at this revelation.

"Mmhnm—ah, Tama. Good morning."

Just at that moment, Aria wakes up. Rising slowly to not wake Vulcan, she smiles down at Tama between her breasts and kisses him on the forehead.

"Meowr—!!"

*Look how it pleases my master—my hands are tied here...* These are the excuses Tama repeats in his mind to convince himself as he rubs his face against Aria's breasts to show her his deepest affection.

"Ooooh…Tama, you are such a remarkable lover boy."

Aria's face flushes red, and her breath is a bit ragged. Tama, knowing the facts behind his evolution, is in high spirits.

As a result, he can accept Aria's fetish, and today he rubs up against her even harder.

Watching the two of them flirt, overlooking the fact that they are actually human and monster, you'd think you were watching two lovers intertwined in the softest embrace.

Warm, fuzzy—fuzzy, warm, lovely…

One fine afternoon—Tama is ensconced between Aria's breasts, as per usual.

They're on the main street in Labyrinthos's mercantile district. Today they're taking a break from adventurer activities, so Tama isn't wearing his protective gear, and Aria isn't equipped with armor or weapons—she's wearing a white blouse and a knee-length black skirt, both with light frills. On Earth, this is known as an outfit that will "kill virginity dead."

Aria's highly revealing adventurer outfit is super attractive, but the neat and clean aura she's giving off through today's getup matches her looks perfectly and is absolutely charming.

As a bonus, her melons—a certain point of pride for Aria—are going wild underneath her blouse, bouncing back and forth, and the sheer gap between them and her mature outfit is creating a truly erotic situation.

"Tama, what do you want to eat tod—? Wait, what's that gathering of people about?"

As she stares at a line of food stalls and is about to ask Tama what he wants for lunch, a group of people enters Aria's field of vision. And just beyond them, she can hear an angry, exploding roar.

"I have a bad feeling about this, Tama. Let's check it out."

"Meow!" *You got it, master.*

Hearing Aria, Tama jumps lithely out from her breasts and lands on the ground. Aria makes sure he's fine before rushing toward the throng, and Tama follows.

"You little shit-for-brains! This beggar scum had the gall to bump into me!"

"He's the perfect punching bag!"

"Gwah…no…mmmfngh…please!"

An appalling scene unfolds just past the crowd. It's a child, wearing shoddy rags, being beaten to a pulp by two men.

Judging from the child's appearance and the conversation, bumping into the man with dirty clothes on has provoked his wrath. The onlookers are concerned and watch the scene unfold with pity, but nobody tries to stop them. Getting wrapped up in such a troublesome affair is too much to ask of these folk.

"Stop it right now!"

A delicate and pleasant voice, yet one certainly filled with rage, erupts through the crowd—of course, it belongs to Aria.

"Who the hell are you—? Wow, now isn't this sight…"

"Heh-heh, what an absolute babe."

At Aria's cry for them to desist, the two men turn around, puzzled. The second they see Aria, they laugh lewdly, eyes darting between her buxom chest and perfect legs.

Aria screws up her face. It's because of the way they're looking at her but also because she can smell their reeking breath from where she stands. It's obvious they're drunk, although it's only just past noon.

"What timing. If this rapscallion needs saving, maybe we'll just take her for a spin instead."

"Uwa-ha-ha! That's the ticket! She'd probably moan so good…
Gwa-ha-ha!"

One of the men laughs derisively and reaches out to touch Aria's
hand—but in that instant, a piercing cry suddenly erupts.

Looking closely, an opaque spear has pierced the man's shoulder.

"Meowrn!!" *Try to touch my master? That'll be your last move…*

Tama roars—he's launched a magic ice spear, Icicle Lance, at the
offender.

Trying to touch his master, Aria, with such filthy hands is
absolutely inexcusable. On top of that, witnessing how they committed violence against a child, Tama's knight spirit is ablaze with
the anger of retribution.

"Meowrn!!" *Icicle Lance!*

Tama launches another magic ice spear. This time, he charges it
up for a few seconds and pierces the other man directly.

"Heh-heh, you did say that you wanted to take me for a spin,
right? Well, come on now…?"

"Uw-uwa—!!"

Aria smiles sadistically to threaten them further. The second
man runs like the wind.

"Hey…hey!! Wait for me…"

The first brute, who took an Icicle Lance to the shoulder, trips
from the intense pain and scrambles after his coconspirator.

"Now, now—are you okay there?"

"Ooh…y-yes…thank you—"

"No need to speak. I will fix you right up."

Aria doesn't pursue the escaping men. She prioritizes helping
the wounded child, taking an emergency healing potion from her
garter belt and putting it to the child's lips.

"It…it doesn't hurt. My body's healed… Thank you so much,
pretty lady!"

"Heh-heh, that's such good news. Shall we go together now?"

"Together…but where? I'm a beggar—I don't have anywhere to go."

The child responds to Aria with a quizzical look, and although Aria couldn't tell from her bedraggled appearance, hearing her voice, she can tell she's a girl.

*Master, just what do you have in mind for this girl?*

Tama is as confused as the young girl. Where exactly does Aria intend to take her?

*This must be a church…*

After following Aria for some time, Tama and the girl—he learns her name is Lala on the way—arrive in front of a house of worship.

"Excuse me, Sister, I have something I'd like to ask of you…"

Stepping inside the vestibule, Aria speaks to one of the nuns nearby. After exchanging words in hushed voices, Aria is led toward the back of the church.

"Lala, wait here for us, okay? Tama, stay and watch over her."

With those words, Aria disappears into a room in the back with the nun.

"Wow, Tama, you are so darn cute!"

"Meow!"

Anything to save his master's life. And Tama doesn't dislike being around children, either. He doesn't have a clue what Aria is up to, but for the moment, he's happy to comfort Lala as she plays with him.

He lets her hug him, he chases after her, and he plays hide-and-seek. After he kills time for a while, Aria returns alongside the nun.

"Little Lala, come here, please. Starting today, this is going to be your home, okay?"

"Huh? My home?"

The nun speaks to Lala with a soft smile upon returning, and Lala stares blankly.

*So that's what you're up to, master! What a noble thing you've done!*

Hearing the nun speak, Tama senses what Aria has arranged—as a result of her actions, Lala will be enrolled in care at the church.

Saving Lala was just something Aria wanted to do. But what might happen afterward was problematic—left behind as a street urchin, there's no saying the same thing wouldn't happen to the girl again…

Concerned for Lala's future, Aria was determined to have her live under the care of the church. Of course, such service is not free, or rather, the enrollment fee is anything but a negligible sum. Aria is by no means rich, but she paid for it herself.

The young girl doesn't understand any of this, but when she learns that she will have warm meals and a place to sleep every night, her face widens in a huge smile.

The nun takes her by the hand, and Aria watches Lala disappear into the church while she addresses Tama lovingly.

"Meow!"

Tama answers her with gusto and dives back in between her breasts. Then he tells himself again—he would do anything to serve Aria, who goes to such lengths to pursue righteousness.

One week later—

Walking along the main street of the mercantile district, Aria stretches and exclaims with joy, "Yeah! We killed it today, too!"

"So true, meow! You've really come a long way, Aria, and our coordination is on point!"

Vulcan answers enthusiastically and pumps her fist in the air. At the same time, Aria's melons bounce up and down in rhythm, and Vulcan's apples also bounce noticeably.

The men close by on the street can't help stealing a glance at their displayed cleavage and side boob. Yet there is one man...no, one beast, who looks at them from a completely different angle.

*Wow, what a sight for sore eyes...*

That's right—it's Tama. Surprisingly, he's not being held by Aria but is instead walking close behind her. And just now, he's looking diagonally upward.

In other words...from Tama's viewpoint, he can see directly up inside Aria's short skirt. Her white, perfectly taut skin is wrapped by a black thong—as always with Aria—and Tama savors the salacious way it wedges into her curves, along with the pleasant aesthetic contrast of black on white.

*As a knight, gazing upon my master's flower garden may sound scandalous, but there's no telling when a dangerous gang will fall upon her. This is another crucial part of my duties as a knight!*

And so on and so forth... As always, Tama is making excuses to drink in Aria's body with his eyes.

There's a reason Aria is in an especially grand mood today, and it has to do with the color of the tag hanging between her breasts. It's different than a week ago—it's changed from bronze to silver. In other words, Aria has graduated from D rank to C rank.

Just the other day, she handed Kussman—who was also C

rank—a loss in their duel, although she was with Tama. Adventurers who have animal companions have their abilities evaluated jointly. Also, Aria has defeated many monsters with Vulcan over the past few days, not the least of which was the minotaur.

Her achievements have been recognized by the guild, and only yesterday, her rank went up. Just now, Aria and Vulcan have completed another quest and are on their way back to the guild.

"Meowr? What's that?!"

Merely stepping foot in the guild, Vulcan points something out, puzzled.

Every adventurer present has gathered in front of the noticeboard that displays quests, and they're all looking in the same direction. If it were morning, this scene would be normal given that all new quests are posted at the same time, but it's just past noon... Exactly what is going on here?

"Oh, hi there, Aria and Vulcan. Welcome back!"

"Anna, thank you. We just returned."

Arnold addresses the pair while walking past, and Vulcan immediately points out the flock of adventurers. Tama is still looking on from ground level, and seeing Arnold's bondage suit digging into his (?) body from up close has caused some severe psychological damage.

"Have you heard the rumor that missing persons are on the rise in the neighboring village?"

"Come to think of it..."

"Yeah, I think I heard about it from a customer at my shop."

Both Aria and Vulcan have heard the rumblings to which Arnold is referring. The town of Renald lies one day by horse carriage from Labyrinthos, and a not-insignificant number of missing persons have been reported there recently...

"Does that mean the notices posted are to find missing persons?"

"No, not quite, Aria. Actually…the postings concern eyewitness accounts of a number of monsters and some *demons* that they are accompanying at a ruin site near Renald."

""—?!""

Aria and Vulcan collectively gasp, eyes wide as saucers.

*What?! Demons?! That means…*

Tama is equally surprised and formulates a theory.

Demons are the progenitors of monsters. They have the power to control the minds of a certain level of monster, and they feed on human flesh.

In other words—

"Did the missing persons from Renald fall into the demons' hands…?"

"Yes, it was feared they were abducted—and now…it's almost guaranteed, Aria."

Arnold answers with downcast eyes and a sorrowful expression.

"Oy! Who's going to take on this request…?!"

"The hell's wrong with you? You're talking about demons here! I feel for the people of Renald, but there's no way I'm going."

All the adventurers gathered in front of the noticeboard are having the same conversation. The quest is to defeat the demons and the monsters accompanying them.

Aside from the ability to control other monsters, many demons are born with extremely powerful skills. Facing such fearsome adversaries, it's no surprise that a regular adventurer would hesitate, no matter how good the pay.

But among them—

"Anna, please tell me the details of the request."

Aria whispers quietly.

"Meowr? Aria, you can't be serious…!"

"Are you for real, Aria?"

"Yes. I might not be strong enough alone. But if we can drive the demons away, we'll prevent further tragedy… I cannot forgive them!!"

*Master…!! It's true after all—that you want to become a person who is strong and righteous, just like the Sword Saint… It will be a dangerous quest, but if my master accepts it, all that's left for me is to fulfill my duties as a knight!*

Aria's gaze is piercing as she spits out her words. Seeing this, Tama is convinced, and he remembers something all over again— the absolute sense of honor filling his master, the one he has sworn to protect.

"Well meow, if that's the case, then I'll take on this quest, too!"

"Vulcan! Are you sure?"

"Any girl who gives up when her partner shows such courage isn't long for this world. It's my duty to be supportive when the times get rough!"

Vulcan speaks with conviction. She also has a heart of gold; Tama can tell.

"Okay, then! As far as the quest details go, because it's a request of this nature, there will be an accompanying knight squadron—"

"Allow me to elaborate on that part."

As Arnold begins to explain the quest, someone suddenly appears and cuts him off.

"Hey now, Anna. Vulcan, it's been quite some time. And, Aria, it's a pleasure to meet you. My name is Cedric Ruiné. I'm one of the knights assigned to accompany this quest. I hope we can all get along."

Cedric is a young man with reddish-brown hair and

emerald-green eyes. He's tall, with a long, thin nose and a brisk smile on his face. He's definitely what the girls would call a hunk.

"Hey now, Cedric! Pretty big deal for the knight squadron leader to turn up himself—what's going on?"

"I'm here to ascertain the level of aspiring applicants. I need to know who is really prepared to put their life on the line."

Cedric looks at Arnold and answers with a positively smoldering, handsome smile. Watching the scene unfold, Aria opens and closes her mouth like a stunned fish.

*What?! That's...Cedric Ruiné?!*

Tama is equally shocked, eyes as round as pie dishes.

Cedric Ruiné... His name is somewhat—rather, exceptionally famous.

Not long ago in this world, there was a massive battle known as Ragnarok between humanity and an army of demonic hordes. The conflict was fiercely violent, but thanks to the service of one man known as the Grand Wizard, humanity came out victorious and restored peace to the land.

Cedric Ruiné is one of the heroes who led humanity to victory, fighting alongside the Grand Wizard, who is also his brother-in-law. Although they are both knights, Cedric is well-known as a hero—of course Tama is aware of him, and it's no surprise that Tama is in shock seeing Cedric stand before him.

"O-oh, it's such an honor to meet you, Mr. Ruiné!!"

Aria finally opens her mouth to speak. Her expression is one of true respect. That should also be a given—in fact, while Cedric is a knight, he's also the eldest brother of the house of the feudal lord who runs Labyrinthos—the Marquis Estate.

There is a *specific reason* he hasn't inherited the estate as head of the family, but that doesn't affect his standing. Yet this is the man who's sworn to protect others as a knight and has made such great achievements that everyone knows him as a hero.

Aria, with a righteous heart herself, has no reason not to be absolutely enamored with him.

For the record…Cedric's brother-in-law, the Grand Wizard, is the "magic-wielding girlie-boy from another world" Vulcan previously mentioned…but Aria doesn't know that yet. Let's leave that alone for now.

"Ha-ha, please call me Cedric, Aria. We're going to be fighting together soon—best to be on a first-name basis."

Aria looked nervous when she addressed Cedric, but he replies coolly.

*Hmm. He is theoretically putting on airs, but I don't sense any disagreeability to him. This must be what they mean by an actual hunk. Absolute night and day from Kussman.*

"Okay, are there any other adventurers who will take on this quest? If not, I will close the entry here and now."

Having finished greeting Aria and company, Cedric turns to the group of adventurers gathered in front of the noticeboard and addresses them in a calm voice that still rings clear.

Each adventurer casts their gaze downward. None of them is willing to sacrifice their own lives to help others, like Aria.

"Okay, then. I'm not seeing anyone else, so I will explain our objective. Standing here won't do—let's head over there and sit down for a talk."

Cedric doesn't even feign to put blame on the adventurers averting their eyes, turning instead to Aria and her friends while suggesting they move to the bar and escorting them there.

Forcing someone into a quest simply opens the possibility of being deserted just when the battle gets ugly, and that will not stand—Cedric knows this full well. He is a hero, after all.

"Okay, where shall I begin? The purpose of this quest—"

Cedric sits down and immediately begins laying out the details outlined on a piece of parchment. It has a summary of the quest written on it:

- Quest objectives: defeating the demons and the monsters controlled by them.
- Quest dispatch: headman of Renald.
- Accompanying members: five, including Cedric.
- Departure: tomorrow morning.

Additionally, because this is expected to be a dangerous endeavor, a very handsome sum is listed for terms of payment.

"Excuse me, Cedric, I have a question…"

"What is it, Aria?"

"Is going up against demons and an unknown number of monsters really advisable with just us?"

*Yes, I was just thinking the same thing. Even with the hero Cedric with us, our numbers make me extremely anxious.*

As Aria asks hesitantly, walking on eggshells, Tama can't help but share her unease.

However—

"Ah, if that's what you're wondering, it's no problem. The four who will accompany me are all first-rate squadron members— men who fought in the Great Demon War and lived to boast about it… And at any rate, I have an ace in the hole, should we need it."

Cedric explains coolly and smiles at the end, giving an impression of absolute confidence.

"Heh-heh, don't worry, Aria. If Cedric really turns it on, he's unstoppable."

Arnold chimes in after Cedric. He leans up against him as he does and intertwines his hand in Cedric's.

"Stop, Anna. You promised you wouldn't do anything like that in front of people, remember?"

"Oh, Cedric, you are so bad."

Cedric pokes Arnold on the cheek and reproaches him in a sweet tone.

Arnold responds in his telltale loving yet husky voice and looks elated.

*Ohhh...are these two...that sort of...?*

Watching Cedric and Arnold interact, Tama and Aria both start imagining...

In other words, the reason Cedric didn't inherit the estate as head of the family is...

But let's leave that alone for now.

Cedric is a hero with uncompromised confidence, and he has Arnold's seal of approval. There shouldn't be any problems with this plan.

While watching Arnold and Cedric grind up on each other, the party officially accepts the quest. It's decided—they'll leave Labyrinthos first thing tomorrow morning.

*Sir Cedric...you are extremely handsome and an upstanding gentleman... You're an aristocrat and leader of the knight squadron—extremely high status. What an absolute shame.*

Such are Tama's thoughts.

"Oof... Okay, Tama. Let's go."

"Meow!"

Early morning—

After finishing changing her clothes, Aria turns to Tama, sitting on the bed like a li'l chonk, and opens her bosom to him.

Tama mews eagerly and leaps from the bed into his regular place, softly ensconced between Aria's melons.

*Hmm?*

Tama realizes something. Aria is squeezing him even more tightly than usual, and her expression is stiff.

*I see—my master is anxious, it seems. I can't blame her—this quest may prove leagues more dangerous than anything she's ever seen before. And accompanying us will be subordinates under the direct control of one Cedric Ruiné...a man who can certainly be called a hero by anyone's reckoning. Okay—it's up to me to assuage my master's anxiety.*

"Meow—"

Tama mews quietly and climbs to the top of Aria's bosom deftly, careful not to scratch her with his claws, and licks her cheek.

"Wha—? Tama, you make me so ticklish. Hee-hee, are you maybe trying to cheer me up because you can tell I'm nervous?"

"Meowr—!!"

Recently, Aria has essentially learned to understand what Tama is trying to say, just from his mewing and actions. Seeing that she responds with the same sweet smile as always, Tama nods in satisfaction.

"Take this as a reward for cheering me up."

It happens so suddenly. So suddenly that Tama doesn't even understand what has transpired for a moment. Yet, when he feels the crush of warmth against his mouth, he knows—Aria's lips are quietly pushed against his.

*Master...*

For Aria, putting her lips to her cat (at least, Tama mistaken as a cat) isn't such a big deal. But for Tama, who on the inside has the consciousness of a fully grown knight, taking a kiss on the mouth from the stunning elf girl standing in front of him is an absolutely astounding occurrence.

*Lub-dub—*

Tama's pulse quickens ever so slightly.

*What is this heart throbbing—?!*

Tama is perplexed. Before he realizes it, in his heart of hearts, Tama is looking at the girl in front of his very eyes not as someone he's devoted to protecting as escort—he sees her through the lens of love. That is why his heart is throbbing.

*...No, this is not the time for such thoughts. I should only be focused on protecting my master to the very end, as a knight!*

In his previous life, Tama was quite introverted. Even now, after reincarnation, that hasn't changed. For this reason, he wasn't even aware of the love awakening in his own heart.

He will quell the longings of his heart through unselfish and chivalrous dedication and give preference to his duty as a knight.

Well, really...Tama's desire to protect Aria will undoubtedly reach a new zenith, but he is certainly unaware...

"Meowr, Aria, good morning meow!"

"Good morning, Vulcan!"

As Aria and Tama arrive at their planned meeting spot, the south gate of Labyrinthos, Vulcan waves and calls out to them, having arrived early.

Aria responds and jogs over to where Vulcan stands.

"Well, well. I guess we're the last ones here."

As Aria arrives at Vulcan's side, she hears a soothing voice call out from behind her. It's Cedric. Compared with yesterday, he's now wearing light armor and has a sword equipped. Four of his knights, a small group of men and women, are waiting behind him.

"Okay. Let me begin by having everyone introduce themselves. Danny, you begin."

"Yes, Captain! My name is Danny. I'm officially second-in-command of this squadron. Pleased to meet you."

Danny has closely cropped hair and introduces himself sociably. He's equipped with light armor and a sword, just like Cedric.

"Allow me to introduce myself next. My nickname is Howard, and I'm a tank, but I am also proficient in hand-to-hand combat. You can count on me!"

Howard is wearing heavy armor and is a big boy, carrying a shield as tall as he is. However, he's not a normal human.

His skin is covered in green scales, and his head is positively reptilian. He is what's known as a lizard man. Just like elves and the tiger-eared clan, he's a species of demi-human.

Next, two female knights come to the front.

"My name is Keni. I'm a specialist with this here battle-ax!"

"My name is Marietta. I wield this *bo*. It's a distinct pleasure to meet you."

Keni raises her ax, voice rife with enthusiasm. She has red hair in a ponytail and sharp reddish-brown eyes. Her equipment includes what qualifies as armor but leaves a lot of skin exposed... She's wearing what is known as bikini armor.

Compared with Keni, Marietta hesitates to even say her own name. Her hair is a short-cut bob, nearly black but closer to indigo blue. Her eyes are also dark indigo. She's wearing the same bikini armor as Keni.

*Hmm, so Howard is the tank, Cedric and Danny are the vanguard, and judging from their equipment, Keni and Marietta are critical sneak-attack specialists... Altogether, they're a bit front heavy, but it's not a bad formation by any means. And this is all on top of the "ace in the hole" Cedric mentioned yesterday, too.*

The knights finish introducing themselves. Tama looks at each of their weapons and ascertains their battle formation immediately. At the same time, seeing knights in their regalia for the first time in ages, Tama feels very nostalgic.

"My name is Aria. I'm a C-ranked adventurer specializing in knives. And this is Tama. He's an elemental cat and still a kitten, but he has powerful innate skills."

Aria greets the knights after their self-introductions finish. It appears Vulcan already knows the crew, so she simply says hello. Then, as Aria finishes introducing Tama...

"W-wow, an elemental cat—how rare. And with innate skills..."

"Wah—he's so cute!"

"Hey, Aria, can I hold him for a minute?"

Howard puts his hand to his chin and stares at Tama with deep intrigue.

Marietta and Keni are already making requests to cuddle the adorable Tama.

Danny gets a glimpse of Aria's cleavage and Vulcan's side boob and immediately looks like a hot mess.

"Well, well, why don't we continue on in the horse carriage, in that case?"

Watching things unfold, Cedric laughs sarcastically and pushes everyone to keep moving forward. A single large horse carriage has been prepared for them. It will take a day's journey to reach Renald.

*Heh-heh, I'm relieved everyone is so friendly. I might just forget that I'm a devoted knight, myself.*

Aria, seeing the knights' casual interactions and manner of speech, forgets all about her own anxiety, too.

"Um...are you sure it's okay? Should I really be relaxing in the carriage like this...?"

Aria hesitates to speak out inside the carriage—for Cedric, the captain of the squadron and an aristocrat, is working as coachman while Howard and Danny follow alongside as lookouts on two spare horses. Inside the spacious transport are only Aria, Tama, and Vulcan, alongside the bikini armor–clad Keni and Marietta.

"It's fine, Aria. Lookout duties work alternately, and the captain is just…the captain, you know?"

"Yeah, it's so true—what a waste, even though he's smoldering hot."

Keni and Marietta look dejected as they answer Aria. Their despondency is not aimed at Aria but rather at their captain, Cedric.

Both Aria and Vulcan have some knowledge of how to maneuver on a steed or run a horse carriage. They rushed to try and stop Cedric, who immediately went to sit in the coachman's seat…

"Ah-ha-ha, don't worry about it, either of you. I like it outside. I can't be in such close quarters breathing the same air as all you women for very long—no thanks."

Cedric rattles off with his trademark refreshing hunk smile. It would appear that not only does he play for the other team, he doesn't even fancy women much at all.

Any girl on the street would do a double take, that's how good-looking Cedric is… Just as Marietta said, it's a definite waste.

"By the way, Marietta, it's time for you to give him up already."

"What are you talking about, Keni? I just switched a minute ago."

Tama is ensconced in between Marietta's breasts poking out from her bikini armor. Keni and Marietta have been waging war on whose turn it is to hold the adorable Tama since the ride began.

Tama being Tama, the touch of Keni's and Marietta's bare skin feels so damn good, he's barely conscious.

What's more—both girls have ample bosoms the size of ripe peaches, and every time the horse carriage hits a bump, they jiggle up and down, the sensation rippling through Tama—yes, they're both really driving the spurs on this exceptionally comfortable ride.

Of course, the only reason he can be so calm in another girl's arms is because Aria commanded it.

"Mmm...I love holding Tama, but watching Tama being held by you is really getting me hot and bothered..."

*Meowr—! Aria, you really do love Tama. Well, you were already a furry, and then he saved your life, so it's not like I don't understand why. Me too, in reality...*

Vulcan can't help but muse to herself as she sees Aria, eyes ablaze watching Tama being held in such rapture by Marietta.

In that moment—

"What meow? The carriage stopped."

"Maybe it's monsters?"

The carriage stops on a dime; Vulcan reaches for her gauntlets and Aria for her knives. Meeting monsters along the road is par for the course.

"Everyone, it's a horde of orcs, but stay put. Danny!!"

"Yes, Captain!"

Cedric speaks to everyone inside the carriage. Just as they expected, the group has encountered some monsters. However, Cedric holds Aria and Vulcan back, instead giving instructions to Danny.

Aria and Vulcan stare out the window and see that several orcs are rushing directly toward them.

"Hey! Look, swine—over here!!"

Danny yells, provoking the orcs while jumping off his horse. Orcs are dim-witted, but they have some manner of intelligence. They become enraged at Danny's taunting and surge toward him.

"Ha-ha, orcs are such simple cretins!!"

Danny is now surrounded on all sides, but he gets a running start and slides directly between one of the orc's legs.

The orc's body shudders, and in that second, it erupts in a blood-curdling scream—"*Snort—!!*"—before falling to the dirt. Looking closely, it's clear one of its legs has been ripped off.

Danny grips a bloody longsword in his hand. He managed to slice one of the orc's legs off while sliding between them.

"Incredible! What a stunt... Is that a special skill?"

"Ha-ha, what are you talking about, Aria? Danny doesn't use skills."

Aria unconsciously gasps, amazed by Danny's dexterous combination of evasion and attack, but Keni laughs lightly at her question.

Then Danny puts the death blow to the incapacitated orc, and next, it's his turn to attack. He steps in, and though the movement looks small, he covers an incredible amount of ground. The orcs recoil and scream in shock at how quickly he closes in on them.

"Okay, now!"

Danny jumps into the air and does a flip over the orcs, accompanied by a dry snapping sound. When he touches back down—two of the orcs' heads are rolling on the ground.

This time, Aria definitely saw exactly what happened—including the second that Danny lopped off both orc heads while flipping over them in midair.

Only two remain—one of them grips a *bo* and swings it down toward Danny.

"Too slow, chump."

Danny speaks coolly and twists his body to evade the strike. The orc has lost its balance from whiffing, and Danny kicks it in the leg, knocking it to the ground before piercing it directly through the heart from the back.

The last orc rushes Danny from behind, but by then, he's already removed his sword again. With his back facing the orc, he rocks it in the solar plexus with the hilt of his weapon, turning around as the orc recoils.

Danny slashes through the orc's torso on a perfectly level plane and watches its body fall in two halves.

"Amazing…this is the power of second-in-command to the captain."

"Meowr, he's another hero himself!"

Aria and Vulcan can't help but voice their wonder.

*Hmm. Slicing an orc completely in half without any skills. To boot, he's rushing all over the place without breaking a sweat… He's fought at Ragnarok and lived to tell about it—for certain.*

Danny returns to his horse like nothing has happened.

Tama, a knight of a similar ilk, is rocked to the core.

*I can't wait to see the other knights fight now!*

"Ah, to thee royal knights—thank you so much for coming here."

It's evening—after they finished their day-long haul. The town headman exclaims, "How we awaited thee!"

Thankfully, the party did not encounter any other monsters after the orcs.

"Let's dive right in—can you please show us the ruins and other places demons have been sighted and explain the situation in detail?"

"Of course, my pleasure. The ruins are only a few minutes

from town. Regarding the missing persons, in fact just last night, another young girl…"

The headman accedes to Cedric's request.

There have already been additional casualties. Aria's arm flexes as she holds Tama. Her heart is in agony for those sacrificed.

"…In reality, we should have been more vigilant from the start, but in any case, our town is still newly founded, and we didn't have a chance to invest in our own protective measures."

"I see. It's true that this village is located on the former site of a demon colony."

Hearing the headman's words, the lizard man Howard whispers to himself, as if recalling the past.

This town—Renald—was founded rather recently at this site, where a demon colony was annihilated by a group of brave knights during the aforementioned Ragnarok. What's more, because Labyrinthos, which has knight squadrons and the Adventurers Guild, is located close by, Renald itself has very weak defenses.

"Now, now—everyone, you must be very tired. Please come this way. We've prepared the inn and hot springs for you, free of charge."

After confirming the distance to the ruins on a map and the types of monsters that have been sighted, the town headman gestures toward the party.

As they bid farewell, the party once again instructs the townspeople to refrain from going outside at all, to the extent possible.

"Damn! This meat is delicious!"

"These deep-fried mountain vegetables are also legit!"

Danny and Howard can't help but tell the whole world how

good the food is at the inn's restaurant. The dishes are meat and mountain vegetable focused. According to the girl running the establishment, in addition to the ruins, there's a small mountain near the town, making for a ready supply of fresh food.

"The booze really goes down easy when the food's so good—!"

"Take it easy there, Marietta. Our task of defeating demons is waiting tomorrow."

Keni cautions Marietta, who sits across from her and is drinking like a fish. Their captain, Cedric, looks at his four knights with a wry smile on his face.

"Maybe it's just me, but they don't seem nervous at all."

"You're right meow. I guess those of the ranks that lived through Ragnarok are simply cut from a different cloth, hey meow?"

Aria and Vulcan are seated in the corner, quietly exchanging opinions.

*Hmm. What to make of this? Seeing them like this, their disposition is closer to adventurers than actual knights.*

Seeing the way they handle themselves and interact among one another, Tama has fostered this impression of the group since they met.

And then...

"I've gotta know right meow—!"

Aria and Vulcan start asking the knights all the questions on their minds.

They've fought at Ragnarok and lived to become heroes... Aria and Vulcan are dying to know what circumstances brought them to become knights.

"What the—? Are you and yours really that curious about such a thing, Aria?"

"We don't mind sharing, but it's really not an interesting story, ya know?"

Having imbibed, Danny's and Howard's faces are red as they reply.

Aria says that she absolutely wants to hear it, and Danny relents: "Okay—I'll start.

"I was born in a poor home. One day, I borrowed money from a bunch of lowlifes. They put an absurd amount of interest on it, and I couldn't pay. I was up against the wall, and my mother was prepared to sell herself to them…"

Around that time, a squadron of knights just happened to stop by Danny's hometown on an excursion. Further, the troop happened to be looking for young, capable hands. Danny already had his wits about him when it came to swordsmanship.

"I was still a kid, and I challenged one of the knights in a duel, expecting to die an honorable death. I told them to hire me as a knight if I won. Told them to pay my wages up front and take care of the entire debt I'd put on my family. Of course, I thought they'd snort through their noses laughing at me, but one of the knights was a real maniac and took my challenge."

In the end…as expected, Danny lost. But it wasn't a lopsided fight.

The captain of the knight squadron went so far as to actually hire Danny. In other words, they shouldered his entire debt.

"If something like that happened to you, you'd agree—you have to pay that person back, no matter what the cost. So I trained harder than ever before and eventually became the first squadron's second-in-command. I had no idea I'd be sent into the gaping maw of Ragnarok, though! Ba-ha-ha-ha-ha!"

After finishing his story, Danny laughs like nobody else is in the room.

"……"

Aria falls silent. Speaking of the first squadron, she's heard that only the highest-ranked knights are placed there. She always thought they were aristocrats like Cedric, but in reality, a regular commoner with deep concern for his family also became one…?

"I was also born a commoner, like Danny. I became a knight for the same reason—to clear my family of debt."

"I also became a knight to have the cost of my ailing older sister's medicine paid for."

"I became a knight under the condition that they would save my father, who'd been forced into slavery."

After Danny, Howard, Keni, and Marietta all chime in.

"Meowr, this is way heavier than I expected. We're so sorry to have asked so lightly…"

Vulcan nods awkwardly, and her tiger-eared-clan ears, normally a point of pride, droop.

"Whatever. Don't look like that, you two!"

"That's right. We have all repaid our debt of gratitude to our knight squadrons, and we're here following orders of our own accord."

Seeing Aria and Vulcan looking gloomy, Danny and Howard have the kind sense to return to addressing them like nothing's happened at all.

After Danny finishes, Keni and Marietta continue.

"Well, the only reason I was able to return all the money the knight squadron lent me is thanks to Captain Cedric's little brother."

"That's right! Little Maiya… Right now, he must be enjoying the harem life with Sakura and them, eh?"

Hearing what Keni and Marietta have to say, Aria reacts with sheer excitement.

"Yeah, he's incredible! Maiya...you're that close with the Grand Wizard? ...And just what does it all mean? You're saying thanks to the Grand Wizard? Wait? And what about Sakura?"

She's more than excited—hearing the name Sakura, which she knows, Aria is now completely flabbergasted.

"Meowr? Aria, you didn't know? Sakura got pregnant by Maiya, meow."

"Ehhh?! You never said a thing about that, Vulcan! Does that mean that you, too, can call the Grand Wizard by his first name?"

"Meow...come to think of it, I told you before about a boy who uses magic, right? Well, Maiya was a regular at my shop before he was ever called 'Grand Wizard.' For the record, I was the one who taught him how to use a staff, too. Wow...it's so meow-stalgic...!"

"Wha—?!"

The strongest young man, who saved the world—the Grand Wizard. A member of Aria's own party, Vulcan, is an old friend of such a person.

Aria faces the greatest shock she's experienced thus far in life.

"The only reason we were able to pay back the knight squadron is because we went on a massive quest with Maiya, who had just come to our world. He split the payment with us."

"Maiya was extremely tough, and a boy with a heart of gold. And he was already strong then—but becoming so strong, he could take out the demons as a lone knight? That's simply astonishing."

*This Maiya took out every last demon all by himself? So the rumor is true. What's more, these honorable knights all idolize him... Someday, I certainly want to meet the legendary Grand Wizard.*

A high level of elevated strength and an elevated persona.

As a former knight, Tama puts great emphasis on these two qualities.

The Grand Wizard likely fulfills them better than anyone else. Tama again wishes to see him even for a moment someday.

The party also asks Cedric his reasons for becoming a knight.

"I don't love women, so I can't inherit my family estate. I became a knight because I was bored. And as a knight, I can not only kill monsters, but if someone is a criminal, I can legally kill them, too. What more could you ask for?"

The party receives a really messed-up answer juxtaposed with Cedric's trademark hunk smile.

Aria and Vulcan are absolutely floored.

The room had been filled with an emotional aura, but Cedric made a mess of it.

"Mmm!"

Aria grabs her shirt and rips it off in one go, revealing her heavy, ripe melons that bounce up and down animatedly. She's in the ladies' changing room for the inn's hot springs.

The innkeeper encouraged Aria and the girls to take a bath after they finished dinner, so they've convened here to rest their travel-worn bodies.

Vulcan is also stripping down next to her, alongside the bikini armor–clad Keni and Marietta, revealing their beautiful exposed skin.

Vulcan has apples, and Keni and Marietta both have peach-size bosoms. They're all gorgeous—a true spectacle of resplendent beauty.

*Oof—my master is one thing, but seeing all these ladies so exposed is absolutely uncouth for a knight. But what can I do?*

Of course, Tama accompanied them. Hearing they'd be going for a hot springs dip, Tama knew that Vulcan and everyone would be there, too, and turned to leave and wait outside, but Aria caught him and put an end to that.

What's more—she told him that he better be a good boy or she'd have her way with him. What else can he do but obey her every command?

"Okay, Tama, time to get in the bath with us!"

"Meow—!!"

Aria's removed her panties and stands as naked as the day she was born, legs spread as she addresses Tama. Her porcelain-white skin is as flawless as ever. Simply beautiful.

On the tips of her breasts, her ideally sized sakura-pink nipples are fresh and bright, perfectly highlighting the depths of her beauty.

Tama leaps onto her breasts, and before he knows it, he's ensconced between them.

"First, we have to wash up alllll over, okay?"

Aria addresses Tama as they enter the washroom. She sets him down and picks up a bar of soap, lathering him in a cloud of suds.

"Huh—even though he's a cat, he doesn't hate getting washed?"

"Tama is so cute covered in soapy bubbles!"

The stark-nude Keni and Marietta are watching Tama while he calmly receives his wash. Completely unabashed, since only girls and a cat are present, they're not wearing towels. To that end, Tama is taking in their nude bodies with abandon.

Fully surrounded by the resplendent flower gardens of so many nude girls, Tama's little behemoth threatens to become a full-fledged behemoth, but if that happens in front of Aria, she won't be able to stop herself from attacking him. Tama controls himself through some form of cold reason.

"…Hmm? What's the matter, Vulcan? What are you doing over there?"

While washing Tama, Aria notices Vulcan watching them from the corner. It's clear she's touching herself *there* and rubbing her thighs together—her face is flushed pink.

"Meow! I-it's nothing. Don't worry about me-ow."

Vulcan replies in a panic. Her voice cracks, and she's staring at Tama lustily.

*I—I can't say it. I didn't know I would throb this hard at Tama seeing me naked. Even if I was wrong, I couldn't say a word.*

Vulcan is screaming inside… She has been holding a secret, it seems.

Aria looks at Vulcan quizzically but recommences washing her body and Tama's anyway, her melons bouncing up and down the whole time. Keni's and Marietta's peaches are shaking, and although Vulcan looks quite ashamed, her apples bounce and change shape, too.

Tama is doing everything he can to keep his little behemoth from going full monster. He starts counting prime numbers simply in an effort to quell himself.

"Phew—okay, Tama, let's get in, okay?"

Tama continues counting. Aria has finished washing herself and beckons to Tama as she slips her foot into the water.

*Thank god. If we get in the tub, I will be able to at least divert my eyes from my master and her company's bodies.*

Tama responds with a hearty meow and gets into the tub with everyone.

"Oh god…they're floating in the tub…"

"Aria, having boobs on your level is truly a glorious sight."

Keni and Marietta enter the tub next and emit cries of shock... and wonder. Aria's melons are floating in the tub, right next to Tama—strictly from the pressure they're exerting on the water.

"There's nothing really that great about them, ya know? My back is always hurting..."

"Damn, back pain, eh...? Well then, maybe you need a rub!"

"Yeah, let's do it!"

"Yeah, I always wanted to feel Aria's monstrous titties, too!"

"H-hey—wha...? You guys?? Ooh...ahhh..."

Hearing Aria's complaint, Keni, Marietta, and Vulcan all open their hands and fly toward her. Of course, they're all going for her melons.

As Aria's soft, voluptuous breasts are rubbed and kneaded by the tiger-eared-clan girl and female knights, Aria can't help but cry out in ecstasy.

"Ooh...ohhh... No! Tama, help!"

"Meow!" *Just wait, master, I'll help— Hmm?*

As Aria calls on him for help, Tama rushes to stop the three girls. But something's not right. Something about him is...just wrong...

"Wow!! I can hear the most erotic conversation happening on the ladies' bath side!"

"Calm yourself, Danny. Don't get so riled up just from coquettish voices."

"What's with the poker face, Howard? Even though you're in such a slump?"

"What's with you guys? I simply fail to understand what's so great about women."

The men's bath lies just across the wall from the women's.

Hearing Aria's gasps while her breaths come hard and rough, Danny and Howard are aroused, and Cedric—with zero interest in women—looks positively disgusted.

"At this point, we totally have to go over there."

"Go over there? Wha—? You can't be serious, you filthy cretin."

"It's just like you're imagining, Howard. This area is separated into men's and women's sides by a wall, but there's only bushes around the sides. Let me make it easy for you—if we go around the side, we'll be able to spy on them all we want! Come on, Howard—I know you're up for it."

"Hmph. I guess I can't refuse a fellow knight's request."

Howard is quick to jump on board with Danny's plan, despite his grumbling.

The pair sets out on tiptoe... They quickly disappear into the bushes, hoping to get a glimpse of Aria and company's baby-smooth skin...but...

"Meow—!"

""Wagyahhhhhhhh!!""

Danny and Howard erupt in a bloodcurdling scream in response to the cute little mew. Stepping into the bushes, they were mere moments from seeing into the women's bath, but just then, a powerful gale blasts them back.

They're rocked into rough brambles and tumble in a scraped-up heap. The source of the gale may not need explanation—it came from Tama's Aether Howl.

Tama sensed Danny's and Howard's agitating presence creeping over from the men's side with his feral instincts and anticipated their arrival.

Now, Keni and all the girls rush over to see just what's happened and find Danny and Howard, with Tama standing watch. Aria surmises the situation, explaining it to the others.

Although they're already bruised from Tama's attack, Danny and Howard face the additional punishment of Keni and Marietta bashing them over the head.

Sweet Jesus—

"I can sense them."

"Yes. It's about six in total. And they're hobgoblins, out of nowhere... Just what's going on inside, I wonder?"

The next morning—Danny and Howard are whispering to each other as they hide under cover. As they've planned, Aria and company have arrived at the ruins in question.

They've confirmed that hobgoblins—higher-level goblin monsters—are patrolling the entrance. They're about as tall as grown human men, and as opposed to regular goblins, they possess intelligence and are therefore quite troublesome monsters.

"Okay—this is our turn to shine!"

"That's right! Leave the sneak attacks to us."

Keni and Marietta are trying to sell the men on an ambush. Cedric nods faintly in agreement, and the pair rushes out.

Incredible speed—not as fast as Aria when she activates Acceleration, but they're fast enough. And they're not only fast—they're silent. Because they're both equipped with bikini armor, their plating doesn't clank against itself.

Their timing is also immaculate—rushing out during the split second the hobgoblins have diverted their vision.

*Crack!*

Marietta bashes one of the goblins on the back of the head with her metal *bo*. The hobgoblin is battered to death before it even knows what's happened.

On Keni's side, a similar scene has developed. She attacks

with her battle-ax and splits a hobgoblin's head from the cranium down to its spinal cord—she's put it down with a single come-from-behind sneak attack.

"*Gu-gyah—!!*"

Now realizing they're being ambushed, all the hobgoblins stampede toward Keni and Marietta. Hobgoblins wield stone axes, and the one leading their charge swings its down toward Keni.

"I've never seen such a slow attack! Eat this, you scum!"

Keni avoids the strike with ease, stepping in closer to kick the hobgoblin in the crotch.

The powerful attack from her steel leggings causes the goblin to erupt in a bloodcurdling scream.

"*Ga-gyah—!!*"

"Nice try, buddy!"

As the hobgoblin writhes in agony, Keni brings up her battle-ax and sends its head flying in one fell swoop.

"Ah yes, an honorable death, no doubt."

Behind Keni, Marietta is repeating a similar attack. She's aiming for the same spot, too—a hobgoblin's crotch. This time, it faces a direct bash from her *bo*.

Just as the name implies, this death took balls.

"*Gu-gyah—!*"

"*Gu-gigi—!*"

Seeing the power of the two bikini armor–clad knights and their heartless nature, the last two hobgoblins run for the hills.

But they're too slow. The second they try to run, fresh blood gushes from both their chests.

"Well done, Keni, Marietta."

"Indeed—I knew it would be, but that was a perfect ambush."

It's Danny and Howard—Danny with his longsword and Howard with his short sword, which have pierced the hobgoblins through the back.

"Okay, according to the map, there is only one exit, so this means the rest of the monsters have no escape route. Let's rush in and assault them before they have a chance to position themselves."

""""Yes, sir!"""""

Everyone sounds off in unison at Cedric's call to arms. Aria and company take up the rear so as not to cause any delay.

"Are these...invaders? From what I can see, it's adventurers and knights... That means they've discovered I'm ensconced here. I told you to be extra careful when abducting any humans from the town..."

In the deep reaches of the ruins—

—a young demon is muttering in annoyance.

His skin is reddish bronze and eyes bright violet, with a venomous tint to his green hair...

He belongs to the race of demons, the scourge of humanity, that lives off devouring their flesh. This young beast is the specific cause of the recent spate of abductions, and the object of Aria and company's quest is to defeat him.

The demon's violet eyes are fixed on a crystal on the ground. Staring into it, the creature watches Aria and company moving through the interior of the ruins. This crystal is a magic item. Imbuing it with magic allows the user to see what's happening in a predetermined area in real time.

"Shit, just when I was about to launch *the plan*... Was abducting humans a mistake after all? But it was necessary to continue sustaining the monsters. There was no other way."

The young demon puts his hand to his chin and continues to grumble.

"No, it's too late for recriminations. In reality, I wanted to increase our forces…increase our battle strength…but now all we can do is act."

After pondering for some time, the young demon makes a decision. Then he closes his eyes and focuses his synapses.

By manipulating mana, demons can make monsters act according to their desires. To that end, it's going to set the monsters prowling throughout the ruins on Aria and company.

"Let's go for a trial run. I'll make you regret ever intruding on my plan, you peasant humans!"

*"Gru-ruuu—guuu—"*

Aria and company have entered the inner ruins, coming face-to-face with some grotesque beings that have come out to greet them with deep growling.

"This is rare—those must be war wolves."

"And this many of them guarantees that demons are lurking around here."

Seeing the war wolves, Howard and Danny chatter among themselves.

War wolves are wolf monsters with humanoid bodies. However, their characteristics are different from both humans and wolves—they prefer isolation and almost always act alone.

Yet, despite this, the war wolves inside the ruins have gathered into a massive pack. From this, it can be deduced that they are being corralled by demons.

"Okay, everyone, let's proceed as usual!"

"""""Yes, sir!"""""

"Aria, Vulcan, and Tama—look for openings and then attack!"

"""Yes, sir!""" "Meow!"

Cedric rattles off orders, and as his crew follows them, the battle begins.

"You foul beasts! Over here!"

Howard leaps out first. He stomps on the ground and bashes his gauntlets loudly against his great shield.

"""*Rowrrr—!!*"""

The war wolves erupt in a roar and rush toward Howard. The blood surges in their eyes.

*Ohhh—he's activating the skill "Provocation." A true tank that survived Ragnarok, no doubt—he has such valuable skills.*

Tama is impressed. The war wolves didn't fall on Howard simply because he made a clamorous racket with his gauntlets and shield. He activated the skill Provocation, which fans the flames of monsters' internal battle instincts, drawing their attention to himself.

A tank's role is to draw as much enemy attention to themselves as possible to ensure that their compatriots are not injured—that is all.

The leading three war wolves descend on Howard and attack him with kicks, punches, and claw scratches in succession.

"Bwa-ha-ha!! Did you think that would possibly affect me?!"

Howard laughs heartily and blocks every one of their attacks with sublime shield deflections. Their blows rock off his shield loudly, but Howard doesn't even flinch. The lizard man's body is rugged and heavy. Attacks a normal person wouldn't be able to endure would never be decisive against him.

"Here we come!"

"In for the kill!"

It's Keni and Marietta's turn to attack the wolves bringing up the rear. However, the war wolves are still fixated on Howard thanks to his use of the Provocation skill, and they don't notice the two girls. They relieve the remaining war wolves of their lives in no time.

"Ha-ha-ha-ha-ha! I love hearing you cry in agony!"

"Ah, Captain, we're crushing it already!"

From the opposite side, Cedric rains down slashes on the war wolves, his voice and expression completely on fire.

Danny looks at him in astonishment and joins the battle. It would seem the rumors that Cedric is an aberration who derives pleasure from killing are true.

"Meow! Cedric, such incredible swordsmanship!"

"I c-can barely see the path of his slashes…! So this is the power of a hero who survived Ragnarok… Tama, we can't afford to face defeat, not one bit!"

"Meow!" *Of course, my master!*

Aria and company provide support from the outside, and they can't look away from Cedric's swordsmanship, either. For starters, he doesn't waste a single movement. He wields his blade with the least effort required and aims directly for weak spots—he kills every beast with a single blow.

"""Rowrrr—!!"""

"Huh? Captain! They're sending reinforcements!"

"It would seem so. But this time around, our enemies are wielding weapons. Aim for their vitals—!"

"Cedric! Okay, leave it to us. Tama!!"

"Meow!" *You got it, master!*

A new wave of war wolves, this time armed, floods out from the rear of the ruins. Cedric has called for vital point-attacks, but Aria forestalls his command and calls to Tama, who rushes to the front and inhales deeply.

*Aether Howl…might be useful, but it will only buy us time. Instead, let's use this as a chance to show master my power anew!*

"Meowrn!" *Aqua Howl!*

Tama lets loose one of his Elemental Howls, Aqua Howl. His breath, now filled with highly pressurized water, rips into the chests of the approaching war wolves.

*That's not all!*

Tama isn't finished. As he blasts them with Aqua Howl, he turns his neck from side to side. The blast of water breath rips into the chests of the war wolves, mowing them down.

……

Silence falls upon Tama and his companions.

The war wolves lie prone on the ground, water dripping from their wounds. It's clear that every one of them has perished from Tama's single attack.

""""What the—?!!"""""

At this incredible spectacle, gasps of surprise escape the knights and Vulcan.

"T-Tama…? Were you hiding such incredible power from us?"

Aria is slack-jawed, looking at him.

Tama replies with the cutest mew he can muster.

"I-imbeciles! What the hell was that insane attack? Wait a second, look at its fur… A cat that can use skills? It must be an elemental cat…! Argh, I can't believe such a burdensome creature slipped in with those knights…!!"

In the deep reaches of the ruins, the young demon is rife with indignation. He never imagined that the war wolves he gathered over such a long period—as a part of his plan—would be obliterated in a single attack.

And there's more. He's taken Tama, who unleashed the powerful skill, for an elemental cat.

"No—the identity of the cat doesn't matter. All that matters is how we exterminate it. In this case, we may have to let *them* loose, and I might need to make an appearance myself…"

The young demon begins walking, manipulating mana at the same time.

He's calling on a certain group of monsters, sleeping deep within the ruins, to awaken—

"Meow! That was such a shock!"

"Yeah it was! I can't believe Tama has such an incredible skill."

"The elemental cat… I'm again deeply impressed by this creature."

Vulcan, Marietta, and Cedric can't help sharing their impressions, alongside the other knights.

Tama is squeezed in between Aria's breasts, a self-satisfied look on his face.

"I am equally surprised. I didn't know Tama has other innate skills…"

As Aria cuddles Tama, she feels pride in the pet she loves so much, but she is also perplexed by his unexpected level of strength—or rather, her cheeks quickly flush red and her breath becomes ragged as she quickly whispers to herself excitedly, "I can't believe my knight is so strong…" and "If he's this strong now, once he's grown up, he can throw me down with that power and overtake me, doing whatever he wants, for as long as he wants…!"

Tama sighs at Aria, realizing that her erotic switch has definitely been flipped.

"Okay, it's time that we delve deeper. We now know Tama's power, but remain on your gua—!"

*Remain on your guard.* Cedric was about to say as much but stops mid-sentence, eyes wide as saucers.

"Hmm? What is this pressure...?"

"Oh no, something terrifying is approaching...!"

Danny nods in answer to Howard. The other knights, alongside Aria and Vulcan, all have stern looks on their faces. An extreme, palpable level of oppression is emanating from the depths of the ruins.

"Well done—you have defeated my war-wolf corps. But you shall go no farther, humans."

A piercing, cold voice erupts simultaneous to the appearance of the young demon... He has reddish-bronze skin, green hair, and violet pupils oozing an irrefutable desire to kill.

"Well, well, the boss has made an appearance. Just what are you planning, demon filth?"

As the demon steps forward, Cedric addresses him, his expression shifting from his normal sweet disposition to the emotionless stare of a Noh mask.

Demons construct societies and have personal lives, just like human beings. A young demon controlling monsters and acting of his own volition is very unnatural. Cedric needs to know his intentions.

"Sure, why not—I'll tell you. My name is Beryl Astaroth. My objective is...revenge."

The young demon—named Beryl—answers in a low voice conveying his abhorrence.

In response, Keni and Marietta recall something.

"What? You said Astaroth? I remember that name..."

"Yeah, that's the name of the original demon colony that Renald was founded on!"

They both recently learned from the town headman and Howard that Renald was built on an old demon colony. This demon, Beryl, bears the same clan name as that colony.

He said *revenge*. In other words, what Beryl intends to do...

"Mwa-ha-ha... That's right, humans. I am the living heir to the Astaroth clan, which was destroyed some years ago. And now I will exact my revenge by wiping Renald off the face of this planet...!"

"I see how it is. So you weren't planning on simply abducting the townspeople."

"Yes, they were merely a convenient food supply for the monsters under his control."

As Beryl loudly announces his motivations, Cedric and Howard recap what they now know.

Beryl is the only remaining survivor of the demon colony. Now, to exact revenge, he's waited many months and years, growing in size and accumulating war potential.

"My demonic brethren! Annihilate these intruders and raze the town to the ground!"

Beryl's voice explodes, and from the darkness behind him...a number of abominable war cries ring out.

"*Grrra-brawww—!*"

"Wha—? Those voices...they can't be..."

"Yes, there's no mistaking them...trolls!"

As soon as the words have left Danny's and Howard's mouths, they appear—giants over nine feet tall with earthen skin. Trolls are monsters with contorted, hideous faces and giant tree trunks for arms and legs.

They are A-ranked monsters and extremely dangerous.

"T-trolls—?!"

"Meow! And there's six of them! They could easily destroy the whole town!"

Aria's and Vulcan's eyes are wide with shock. They can't believe that Beryl could be in control of this many monsters of such superior strength.

Cedric lets orders fly. "Spread out!! Don't even think of sticking together!"

Trolls have superhuman strength and reach. Grouping together to attack them only increases the party's chances of being felled together.

That's why they have to spread out and attack in a hit-and-run pattern.

"Heh-heh-heh! Here they are! Multi-Protect Barrier!"

The moment the party fans out—Beryl opens his eyes wide and laughs as he activates a skill.

"Damn—what is this?"

"Shit, that's bad news."

Cedric and Danny expound on the unfavorable situation.

Everyone is snared in groups behind opaque barriers. Multi-Protect Barrier is Beryl's innate skill that can extend multiple fortified barriers at once.

The barriers he's created are square, and they've trapped the party in with the trolls.

The knights are trapped in with two trolls, Tama is trapped with four trolls, and Aria and Vulcan are with Beryl.

"Heh-heh…your elemental cat is in the greatest predicament. He's circled in there nice and cuddly."

"You bastard! Tama!!"

Aria screams out in anguish seeing Tama trapped inside the barrier with four trolls.

*Crap!! I left her side and circled around to protect my master, but the tables have turned on me!*

Seeing the trolls lumbering toward them, Tama jumped out from between Aria's breasts and distanced himself from her.

Tama is infinitely more worried about Aria than his own dire situation.

"Yes! Your pitiful deaths will signal the epoch of my revenge!"

*"Grrra-brawwwww—!"*

The four trolls trapped with Tama lunge toward him. They're all equipped with massive axes and hatchets.

"Meow!" *Aqua Howl!*

Tama activates Aqua Howl, his Elemental Howl skill. Just as earlier with the war wolves, he aims it from side to side.

*Rrr-ppplashhh—!*

The trolls' torsos all turn concave from the howl. Yet, unlike the war wolves, their torsos are not severed by the blast.

*Crap! A-ranked monsters are much more resilient…!*

Trolls have thick, tough skin, and their muscle fibers are infinitely more developed than the average monster. For this reason, Tama's Aqua Howl doesn't come close to taking them down in one shot.

The troll erupts. *"Gra-braw—!"*

In that moment, the wounds on their chests begin *healing before Tama's very eyes.*

*Self-regeneration capability… I've heard the rumors, but I've never seen it before.*

Tama recalls information he's picked up along his exploits—trolls not only boast superhuman strength but also the capacity to self-regenerate.

Trolls have the power to convert the mana in their bodies to flesh and heal their wounds. They're immortal for as long as their mana lasts… It's one of the primary reasons they're classified as A-ranked monsters.

*"Grrra-bra-bra-brawww—!"*

The troll that finishes regenerating first swings its hatchet down toward Tama.

*Such an attack would never fell me!*

Tama lunges in a side step and avoids the blow. Missing its target, the hatchet rips forcefully into the earth and leaves a deep impression.

*This will not be enough. I need to unleash more power.*

Tama looks cornered at first glance, but he's not flustered. He gathers air in his lungs and activates a different skill.

"Meowrn!" *Rock Howl!!*

Tama's howl gathers mass and rips deep into the trolls' tough skin.

"Meow!" *Okay, once more!!*

This time, Tama uses Flame Howl, and before the wounds caused from Rock Howl can heal, the trolls' skin is directly scorched.

"*Gra-brawww—?!*"

Self-regeneration or not, the trolls can't block out pain. Now, it reaches peak threshold, and the trolls thrash around violently, their burned skin exposed.

*Flame Howl—!!*

*Flame Howl—!!*

*Flame Howl—!!*

Tama does not cease howling. He completely boxes in the trolls and burns them to a crisp, until the mana fueling their self-regeneration is fully drained.

Ultimately, the very same Multi-Protect Barrier that Beryl had cast was the cause of the trolls' defeat. Had they been in a wide-open area, they would have had a number of routes of escape and a certain path to victory...

"Come now, Captain."

"Leave it to us already."

"Oy, what sort of treatment is that from my underlings?"

Cedric responds incredulously to Danny and Howard.

"What are you talking about? This sort of enemy is right up the captain's alley!"

"Yep! Let him *unleash his power* and obliterate them!"

Keni and Marietta get right on Danny and Howard. Laughing wryly at his subordinates, the leader draws his sword, as if to say, *Yeah, I get it.*

And then...

Cedric quietly chants, "Unleash the power of the dark—"

His longsword glints as black as the abyss. An ominous enchanted power emanates from his blade.

"Now, let's go."

Holding his sword at mid-level, Cedric rushes forward. He slips quickly in between two trolls and slashes into their torsos.

Both trolls cry out in agony. "*Graw-brawwwww—!!*"

The searing pain of being slashed open...or really, the absolute agony of their entire situation.

"Ba-ha-ha—how is it? The feeling of having your very life taken from you."

Cedric speaks with a smile.

The pitch-black shimmering presence swallowing his blade...it is a magical energy of the dark elemental type—what's called the power of the dark.

The dark elements can only be used as an inherent element by the Grand Wizard, who saved the world from extinction during Ragnarok. Its effects allow the user's attack to drain the life energy from the target, ignoring all defenses.

The Grand Wizard is Cedric's brother-in-law, and he imbued the knight Cedric's sword with this dark elemental power—thinking of him as a brother himself.

"We're going to have a great time—at least one of us is...right?"

Cedric laughs sadistically.

*Impossible! There's no way...?!*

Watching his precious trolls be obliterated inside both barriers, Beryl becomes irate.

"Should you really be taking your eyes off me-ow??"

"Shi—!"

Vulcan flies at Beryl with her battle hammer raised. Beryl leaps far to the side and just barely evades her attack.

"Now!"

Aria leaps forward. She's already activated Acceleration, and her speed has reached apex levels.

"Back I say, you shrimp!"

Beryl removes his sword from his waist and deflects Aria's knife.

Demons have a vastly superior muscle structure compared to humans.

Going pound for pound, there's no way Aria can win. That's why she needs—

"Whirlwind Slash!"

Aria activates Whirlwind Slash, and her body is covered in a storm of blades. Just as Beryl steps back, she succeeds in cutting his skin.

"You filthy human scum!"

Beryl curses, highly provoked.

Beryl had assumed that the trolls would have cleaned up Tama and the knights without issue by now—and that he would have easily defeated Aria and Vulcan.

Yet the second the curtain went up, Tama and the knights were vastly stronger than expected, and neither Aria nor Vulcan is a threat alone, but as a cutthroat team, they have him cornered.

*It's not my time yet! If I can just defeat these two, I will prevail!!*

Beryl's Multi-Protection Barrier is a powerful innate skill. Its effects last until the party that activates it cancels it or becomes incapacitated.

Beryl will cancel the barriers after he defeats Aria and Vulcan. Then he will activate them again immediately and trap in Tama and the knights, intending to flee.

He has no other choice at present. Giving up on his revenge, Beryl now turns his focus to simply surviving.

*I'll have all the chances in the world for revenge if I can just get out of here alive. I have to get rid of these scum, no matter what!!*

Beryl has made up his mind. He removes two daggers from inside his cloak and dual wields them.

*Whoosh—!!*

Beryl stretches out his blades from both sides and rushes forward. He's on a one-way track.

"Vulcan! I'll do you-know-what!"

"Got it, meow!"

As Aria and Vulcan converse, Vulcan raises her battle hammer high in the air.

*Imbeciles! How do you expect to hit me with that?!*

Seeing Vulcan lifting her hammer high, Beryl snickers at her and slightly modifies his approach to avoid the path of her attack, evading the battle hammer entirely.

*Do-gwoh—!!*

Vulcan's battle hammer misses the mark and thuds into the earth, sending up clouds of dust.

*Shit! I can't see a thing!*

Beryl's vision is obstructed by the dust storm. This was Aria and her companion's intent all along.

*Zoom—!!*

A single flash rushes through the dust cloud on a straight line. The gleam hones in on Beryl, burying itself in his chest with a hiss—one of Aria's knives.

"*Gu-gyahhh*—you vile…scum…!!"

Beryl lashes out with his daggers in desperation. He comes dangerously close to Aria's upper arm but then collapses in a heap.

"Meow!!" *My master!*

"Tama!!"

As Beryl has been rendered incapacitated, the barriers fall. Tama races toward Aria, who he'd been watching with much trepidation from behind the barrier.

But wait—

The moment Aria stoops to scoop up Tama in her arms, her entire body shudders, and she slumps to the ground.

*M-my master! What's happened?!*

Tama is confounded by Aria's sudden fainting spell.

"Meowr?! This is—!!"

Vulcan is staring at Aria's upper arm.

"What the hell?! Aria has what looks like a small bruise on her arm…!"

The knights all surround Aria. Looking closely, they can see a tiny purple bruise rising from her skin.

"G-gah…m-my…blade…was covered in dragon poison… You will be joining me on this path, girl…"

With a great deal of effort, Beryl manages to string these words together. Having spat this last curse, his eyes open wide, and the breath leaves his body entirely.

"Dragon poison?!"

"We need an antidote right meow!!"

Aria is in pure anguish and loses consciousness.

Cedric and Vulcan hold her in their arms, debating their options.

"But how? Dragon poison antidote requires the eye of an earth dragon, right?! Where in the hell are we going to get it?"

"For starters, we have to get Aria back to Renald right away!"

"Okay, I got it. I will take her."

Howard responds to Keni and Marietta by taking Aria in his arms and racing out of the ruins. Tama is left alone in that place, absolutely stricken with grief.

*An earth dragon... There's no way I can obtain the eye of an S-ranked monster...*

Just as Keni said, in order to cure dragon poison, an antidote must be infused with the eyeball of an earth dragon and given to the infected party.

The situation is dire.

*Earth dragon... Wait, an earth dragon?!*

Tama stops in his tracks.

*I can't just wait here!*

Tama activates his Flight skill and takes to the sky.

An earth dragon—

Tama rushes for the deep recesses of the labyrinth to find the monster that once pushed him to the brink of his own existence.

Through fields, across rivers, flying through the sky—Tama travels for hours before finally arriving at the labyrinth.

"Gi-giii—!"

"Gu-gyahhh—!"

Seeing Tama, a group of goblins raises shrill voices and rushes at him.

"Meowwwrrrn!!" *Get out of my wayyyyy!!*

Tama roars and launches himself through the air, activating Aether Edge and slicing through his foes like butter, leaving them where they fall.

Finally, Tama reaches the deepest recesses of the upper level and finds the opening that leads to the lowest level.

*Just wait, my master. I promise to save you!*

Tama flies downward with unwavering resolve.

"Just what am I sensing?"

On the lowest level of the labyrinth—

The most fearsome being in the entire labyrinth, the S-ranked monster earth dragon, can feel something approaching its head. Blood rushes to its discerning eye.

And then—

*Whoosh—!!*

Tama swoops down in front of the dragon's eye and flutters in midair. His eyes, which normally make him cute as a button, are tense and penetrating.

"Just what do you think you're doing, feeble one? Even though you successfully escaped me once, you now dance back—and for what?"

"Meow!" *This is what!*

As the earth dragon addresses the behemoth silently—though with grave seriousness—Tama puts up zero argument and instead unleashes a Flame Howl directly in the dragon's face.

"Bwa-ha-ha-ha!! What fun!! I will take you on again, yes. And as far as what you did to my eye—I will make you wish you were never born!"

Tama has no idea what the dragon is planning, but it bares its fangs at the sworn enemy that robbed it of sight in one eye.

That's all the motivation the earth dragon needs to eviscerate Tama. It laughs sharply and brings its front claws down on the Flame Howl erupting in its face.

*Gwohhh—!!*

The dragon's claws break through the Flame Howl and rush toward Tama. The dragon's front legs are lightly singed from the blast, but it's not seriously damaged.

*Shit! Even Flame Howl only does that much damage? In that case—!!*

Tama flies hard to the right to evade the earth dragon's claws.

"Gwa-ha-ha… Dodged my attack, did you?"

Previously, Tama was rendered incapable of battle in one fell swoop, but things are different now. Sure, it's just one attack, but Tama has studied the earth dragon's movements, and he is fully attuned to his behemoth body.

He knows he will be seized upon immediately if he fights the dragon on the ground. Tama intends to continue activating Flight and fighting the dragon at high speed in midair.

"Meow!" *Rock Edge!*

Just as he avoids the dragon's attack, Tama activates his earth Elemental Tail Blade skill, Rock Edge. Distancing himself from the earth dragon, Tama aims his powerful attack at its front legs.

"Argh—?! You dare to injure me! Then what of this?!"

Through his earth elemental attack, Tama has succeeded in damaging the earth dragon. In that moment, the beast does a 180-degree turn and lashes out with a blunt tail bash.

*Ugh! I can't escape this! In that case—!!*

Endeavoring to escape the tail bash, Tama determines that he cannot avoid it entirely. The earth dragon has incredible power—being grazed would not be getting off scot-free.

Tama activates one of his absorbed skills, Iron Body. The second the earth dragon's tail is about to swipe him, his body becomes hard as iron and the damage is voided.

Now it's Tama's turn—he chooses another Elemental Tail Blade skill, Aether Edge, and aims for the earth dragon's eye, just like before.

"You fool! I have already seen through your attack!!"

There is no arrogance in the earth dragon this time around. He feels the current of mana emanating from Tama's tail and turns his face away immediately.

*This is going to be a long, bitter battle…*

In one corner, the immensely powerful and ultra-resilient S-ranked monster, earth dragon.

In the other corner, with experience as a knight in his previous life, the highly skilled yet adolescent S-ranked monster, behemoth.

Tama estimates it will be a long and fearsome conflict, with incessant exchanges of offense and defense and a thin line of ebb and flow, life and death.

Just as Tama expects, the fight becomes mind-numbingly intense and has already stretched for almost thirty minutes.

However, something has changed.

"Huff…phew…"

"Gwa-ha-ha… What's the matter, small fry? Out of breath, are we?"

The earth dragon must recognize Tama's capabilities—it's started calling him *small fry* instead of *weakling*. The earth dragon's body is now entirely covered in wounds.

In comparison, because Tama was able to keep distance using airborne combat and defend against any chip damage by using Iron Body, he's largely unscathed.

Yet, just as the earth dragon said, Tama is breathing hard compared to the start of the engagement, and he feels lackluster.

"Just give up. You cannot defeat me. Give in to a quiet death."

*He's not wrong… I have a good variety of different moves, but my stamina is waning. And my mana is nearly depleted. At this rate, I will be defeated. At this rate—that is!!*

Tama can't win, not like this. That's why he's made a decision—he repeats in his heart of hearts…

*Good-bye, my master…!!*

Then Tama pictures something in his mind. The words *evolution possible* that appeared in his status a while back.

*Flash—!!*

Tama's body suddenly erupts in a flash of light. It burns brightly and floods the entire room.

"Gwa—?! What is this infernal light—?!"

The earth dragon unconsciously turns its face away from the blast. The light converges, and what the earth dragon sees standing in front of it is—

A massive body covered in jet-black fur. Two demon-esque horns protrude from its head, and razor-sharp fangs jut from its jaw.

It has wings, which are covered in blue-black armor, alongside its torso and legs.

Put simply, it's a lion with the features of a dragon—the four-legged beast stands, imposing an aura of great majesty.

"What the—?! What the hell are you??"

A four-legged beast has emerged from the ball of light, and the earth dragon is rocked into a panic from the sudden turn of events.

*"Wrrroooarrrhhh!!!"*

The four-legged beast roars. The atmosphere ripples from the incredible volume, and the beast speaks.

"My name is Tama—!! I am the knight of the adventurer Aria and an S-ranked monster, behemoth! In order to save my master's life, I will be taking yours!!"

The jet-black, four-legged beast is Tama—having evolved to the behemoth's second stage.

To save his beloved master, Aria...Tama has made the decision to ascend to the next stage of his life cycle—a behemoth's true form.

*I'm sorry—time is running short. Let me make this easy on you.*

*"Wrrroooarrrhhh!!!"*

Tama roars again, but this isn't just his voice—this roar bears the burning death of hellfire.

Tama has unleashed Flame Howl.

"Gwaaahhh—!! What is this power? I may be finished—!!"

Tama's Elemental Howl skills have greatly enhanced due to his evolution. The earth dragon's skin blisters and peels away before his very eyes. At this rate, it will burn to ashes and perish.

The earth dragon retreats far to the rear, attempting to escape the hellfire, but then—

"You're finished."

The words echo from the other side of the blaze.

*"Bwohhh—!!"*

Rushing through the flames, Tama leaps and lands directly in front of the earth dragon. A massive blade of fire—Flame Edge—has appeared on the tip of his tail.

"Nooo—!!"

The fiery greatsword slices through the air. Realizing it doesn't have time to evade, the earth dragon attempts to mount a counterattack, flailing its claws in a sideswipe.

*Slash—!!*

Tama's Flame Edge and the earth dragon's claws intersect. The earth dragon's attack lands, gouging Tama from face to chest, leaving a large wound. However, Tama deftly dodges in the final second to avoid sustaining any fatal damage.

In the next instant, Tama's Flame Edge rips into the earth dragon's head from the side, cleaving it wide open. Victory has been secured.

In the battle between S-ranked monsters, the champion is Tama.

*I'm not done yet. I have to bring this beast's eyeball to Aria as quickly as possible.*

It's true—Tama's duty doesn't end after slaying the earth dragon. He still has to deliver the monster's eyeball to Aria before she takes a turn for the worse.

Tama is on the brink of collapsing due to his injuries. He tries to collect the earth dragon's corpse using his Storage skill before rising up to fly away…but…

"Guh—what is this?!"

Suddenly, Tama feels like the mana inside his body is heaving in every direction. His body refuses to obey him, rendering him unable to move.

In that moment—

*Flash—!!*

For a brief instant, Tama's body is again bathed in light, which quickly fades. And when the light completely vanishes…

"Meow!" *My body is becoming small again!*

Yes—Tama's body has returned to…its small kitten form.

*But why? Does the evolution have a time limit? Or maybe… No, forget it—I have to return to my master, now!*

Tama doesn't understand why his body reverted to its previous incarnation, but he is grateful nonetheless.

He promptly secures the earth dragon's corpse with Storage, then takes to the air with his injuries to return to Renald as quickly as he can.

"Unghhh…ohhh…Tama…Tama…"

At the inn in Renald, Aria is caught in a terrible nightmare due to the dragon poison. She calls out Tama's name repeatedly, clinging to his comforting existence.

Vulcan squeezes Aria's hand, her face stricken with grief.

"Damn! We have no antidote."

Cedric bitterly spits out the words.

Returning to Renald, they asked the doctor and pharmacist for an antidote for the poison, but their replies were exactly as expected. Neither had any stock of the necessary ingredient for the antivenom—an earth dragon's eye.

In this far-flung rural corner of the world, that is a given.

Betting on a sliver of hope, they searched Beryl's corpse and combed through the ruins he called home, to no avail.

"If only we were of more use…"

"Aria…"

Keni and Marietta whisper to themselves a short distance from Aria's bed. Because they had accompanied Aria when she was laid low, they feel a great sense of responsibility as knights for allowing this tragedy to come to pass.

Danny and Howard can only bring themselves to stare silently at Aria.

But in that exact moment—

"Meow—meow!!"

They hear a cry from outside the window.

"Tama! I was wondering where you were—what are you doing out there?! You're covered in gashes!"

Cedric rushes to open the window and lets Tama in. However, Tama ignores his outstretched hand and jumps onto the floor.

"Meow!" *Activate Storage!*

"What the—? An earth dragon?!"

"Say what—?!"

Hearing Cedric, Vulcan and the other knights poke their heads in to find out what's happening.

Tama's Storage skill has produced the broken skull of the earth dragon and its corpse in the middle of the room at the inn.

"Tama is heavily wounded…and here's the corpse of an earth dragon… There's no way…"

"That is beside the point! Pluck out its eye and synthesize an antidote for Aria!!"

"I'll call the doctor and the pharmacist right meow!"

Danny's eyes open wide in shock for a moment before Howard reprimands him, demanding the antidote immediately. Vulcan rushes out of the inn to find help.

*This is good. This way, my master will be saved…*

Thanks to Marietta and the others still in the inn, Tama receives a potion, and his wounds begin to heal. Now certain that Aria will soon be right as rain, Tama is relieved and quickly falls unconscious.

"Heh-heh, good morning, Tama…"

"Meowr—!!"

Tama awakens between Aria's breasts at the inn in Labyrinthos. Several days have passed. Thanks to the earth dragon's eyeball, Aria's life was saved.

Of course, the defeat of Beryl was deemed a grand success, and now she's just waiting for her payment to come through.

But she's still concerned about one thing. Certainly, her life has been saved, but the virulent toxin that afflicted her had extreme effects, chipping away at her constitution and sapping much of her physical strength.

Due to this, Aria has become very weak, and even now, days later, she is still undergoing medical treatment.

"But really, that earth dragon corpse... Tama, did you...?"

"Meowr?"

And there's one more thing she's worried about—did Tama really defeat an earth dragon and bring its entire corpse back with him?

According to Cedric, the earth dragon corpse appeared at the same time Tama returned—she has good reason to be concerned.

Aria questions Tama multiple times...but Tama simply cocks his head to the side and mews, as if saying, *What are you talking about?*

"Meowrrr—"

"Ohhh, Tama, you are such a baby."

Tama rubs his head against Aria's cheek, ignoring her attempts to uncover the truth.

At this point, her worries are a small matter—because she loves Tama with all her heart, and he has pledged his undying loyalty to her until the end of his days.

It's nice to meet you, everyone.

My name is Aria, and I'm an elf—currently ten years old.

Right now, I'm in a bit of a pinch.

"She went that way! Don't let her get away! Elves fetch a great price!"

"I know! Who'd let easy money like that get away?"

I can hear voices calling out behind me as I run away.

While I was walking around in the woods of the elven homeland Lumilus, a man and a woman suddenly started chasing me, saying they'd "give me candy."

I bolted right away. My mother always taught me that people who say things like that might kidnap me. After overhearing them while they're running after me, I'm pretty sure that's exactly what these two plan to do. If they catch me, I'll definitely be sold as a slave.

That's when I trip and fall.

"Heh-heh, can't run now, eh, girlie? Since you're already down there, how 'bout giving me a *taste* while I'm at it, eh?"

"*Sigh...* Even a kid like this gets you going?"

The kidnappers keep chatting as they come closer. The man pulls his pants down and whips out something nasty.

I've seen something like it before when I used to take baths with my father, who passed away from an illness, but this one is a lot smaller. It's a bit…sad-looking?

Still, the thing seems stiff and almost angry. I've heard about this before. When men feel excited, they end up like this…

In other words, at this rate…

"Let's get this pesky thing out of the way first."

The man exposing himself grips my shoulder hard and reaches for my clothes, tearing them off.

"Stop! Don't! Please, someone, help me—!!"

"Mwa-ha-ha!! Great reaction! This is perfect!"

"Just give up now, girlie. Not like anyone's gonna come for you out here in these woods."

The man looks even more excited after I scream out for help, while the woman seems annoyed, telling me to just accept my fate.

"Okay, first I'm going to lick-lick-lick your pretty little body!"

The man sticks out his tongue and brings it close to my exposed chest.

*No, no…he's going to…*

I don't actually know much about this subject, so I have no idea exactly what this man plans to do, but I know I'm terrified. My eyes well up with tears. My body freezes, refusing to move, and I can't bring myself to fight back even the tiniest bit.

But suddenly—

"Meowrrrn!!"

I hear a voice from behind the man, who screams, "Gyahhhh!!"

Looking closely, I can see something that looks like a see-through spear sticking into the man's back and coming out his chest! He slumps forward onto the ground. Now seeing a massive beast standing in front of me, my eyes open wide.

"Leo!"

"Mrooow!"

I call out the creature's name, and he answers me excitedly. By his tone, I can tell he's asking, *Are you okay?*

This is Leo, a creature known as an elemental cat.

Elemental cats are quite different from normal ones—when they become adults, like Leo, they can grow up to six feet in size. Just like humans and monsters, they can use extraordinary powers called skills. Just now, Leo activated Icicle Lance to attack one of the kidnappers.

"A giant cat that can use skills... There's no— Could it be an elemental cat?! Why the hell are you here...?! You can't be this brat's pet!!"

The remaining kidnapper raises her voice, eyes wide as the moon. She's in complete shock.

She's right, though; Leo isn't my pet. A woman living nearby who plays with me often is the one who keeps him as her hunting partner. Of course, Leo and I have become good friends, too, so when he found me being attacked while on his usual walk, he came to save me right away.

"Shit!"

Glancing at Leo and the man's corpse, the woman dashes off at full speed. Realizing she has no chance against Leo, she's leaving her dead partner behind... I guess there's no honor among kidnappers.

"Meowrrrooownnn!!!"

Leo roars and catches up to the woman in a single leap. He definitely doesn't plan on letting her go.

*That's it, Leo! Teach her a lesson!*

I'm rooting for Leo inside. But there's something I haven't realized—Leo's voice is much more excited than usual, and his beautiful eyes are bulging in their sockets...

Falling upon the woman, Leo strikes her with a vicious cat punch to the back of the head.

"Gyahhhhh—!!"

The woman screams in pain and falls onto the ground.

"Meowww..."

*Oh, what? Is that...Leo's...?!*

I've realized what's happening. Leo's...*thing*...which is usually hidden by his fur, is bigger...and it's growing. Oh wow...it's like a razor-sharp greatsword.

Leo's breath is ragged. His usual gentleness is nowhere to be found.

*Twinge.*

Watching Leo's body heave in excitement for some reason sets my heart racing. What exactly is this feeling?

"Wait...no, don't tell me this elemental cat is—?!"

The female kidnapper sees Leo's special place and yelps. She tries to crawl away, but...*wham!* Leo stomps down on the scruff of her neck with his massive front paws and stops her dead in her tracks.

*Tear! Ripppp!*

Leo proceeds to rip the woman's clothes to shreds with his jaws—her shirt, her skirt, and even her underwear. I'd learn about this much later, but right now, Leo is in heat—basically a certain time when he feels particularly aroused.

Elemental cats are intelligent animals. Normally, they can suppress their urges, even when they're in heat, but according to the woman who owns him, seeing me being attacked riled him up, provoking his sexual desire (?), and he snapped.

"Ahhhhhhhh—?!"

The woman's scream reverberates. Oh my—! Leo's greatsword is going *whoom*...and then *whaaam*...and then...!!"

"Aaaggghhhhh......noooooooo...!!"

With each quick, repetitive movement, the woman's voice erupts. What's happening? She keeps struggling and looks like she's melting into the ground.

Also, something's not right. Watching this makes my heart flutter, and...my body feels like it's...throbbing?

Leo continues until the woman kidnapper passes out. In the meantime, Leo's owner appears and tends to me.

From this one experience, I decide I hate human men. On the other hand, I love the elemental cat that saved me from being kidnapped—or really, just all cats in general—and someday, I might want a cute kitty to do wild things with...? Maybe I do, and then again, maybe I don't?

Hello, everyone.

My name is Aria, and I'm eleven years old.

I'm caught in another pickle today.

Cries of mourning and echoes of misery. Under attack by a demon army, the elf homeland of Lumilus has become hell on earth.

Demons eat people for food, and they are a foul race that revels in murder. On top of that, they're far stronger than elves and are more skilled at warfare.

The elves of Lumilus are being slain one by one—by the sword and by skills.

"Mama...where are you?"

In the confusion of the attack, I lost track of my mother, and I'm hiding from the demons alone in a grass thicket, purely terrified.

"*Snort*—something smells great over this way!"

A demon wielding a sword peers around with bloodshot eyes as he comes closer to the thicket covering me. Demons have amazing senses of smell. This one must have caught my scent, as he soon discovers my hiding place.

"Mwa-ha-ha!! It's a young girl! How lucky—elf girls are the softest, tastiest treat!"

"Oy! Not fair! I want some!"

The demons push through the tall grass, laughing as they thrust their hands toward me. Behind them, other demons shuffle through the brush to join them.

My mind is filled with nothing but fear, to the point that I can't manage to make even the smallest yelp. I'm so scared, I wet myself in the grass right where I sit…

"Mwa-ha… I'll start with your juicy little arm… Huh—?!"

The demon reaching for me cries out in surprise. I am also confused, because the arm the demon was extending toward me has burst into pieces from the elbow down, chunks flying in every direction.

"Waggghhhhhhhh!! My—! My aaaaarm!!"

A moment later, the demon lets out a high-pitched scream as fresh blood spews from the gash where a limb used to be.

"Gyahhhhhh—!!"

"Huh…my leg…?!"

More shouts erupt all around me. I have no idea what's going on. How could I? I can only tell that many of the other demons are now missing torsos, legs, or necks, their bodies dismembered.

"Are you injured?"

"Huh…?"

As I remain completely oblivious to what's going on, a voice rings clear as a bell in my ear. It came from behind me. When I turn around, I notice an elf standing there.

She has long hair that reaches her waist and porcelain-white skin. Her bluish-silver military clothing makes her look like a goddess of war leaped straight out of an ancient myth.

This mysterious elf is so gorgeous that I'm completely entranced, almost forgetting for a split second that I came quite close to getting killed by demons.

The elf holds a silvery bone-white longsword in one hand and a pure-black one in the other. Blood drips from both blades...

"You're safe now; don't worry."

She swings her weapons through the air to clean them of gore before sheathing them with the exquisite grace of a bird folding its wings. Then she strokes my cheek.

I finally understand. This is the person who killed the demons. She saved my life—

The demons fell by her hand, restoring peace to our home.

This is the story of my first encounter with the Sword Saint, Alisha. Meeting her like this inspires me to make a decision. Someday, I will become as strong as she is, a warrior who can save the lives of those who cannot protect themselves...

Thankfully, I was born with the innate skill Acceleration. I've also been trying my best to train my swordsmanship...but it's become clear that I don't have talent with a longsword like the Sword Saint does.

To be blunt, my innate skill, Acceleration, doesn't pair well with longswords. If I had been born with more natural skill in swordsmanship, I could probably activate Acceleration and coordinate the timing of my sword swings to match.

Unfortunately, I never quite managed to do that, which is why I decided to change my fighting style to specialize in speed. That's when I switched to using knives instead.

Turns out that was the right call. Knives are shorter and turn easily in my hands, matching perfectly with my skill set. This success comes with a complicated emotion, though, because for the longest time, I'd dreamed of gallantly wielding two longswords in battle, just like the Sword Saint. But at the end of the day, my goal is to be a compassionate, righteous warrior. I'm not about to let something so minor get me down.

That said…my admiration for the Sword Saint knows no bounds, and I've imitated her by growing out my previously short hair and trying to sound less like a child by speaking more formally, among other things…

As I honed my knife and skill proficiency, I turned sixteen years old. In order to continue my training, I've left my hometown to take on an apprenticeship.

My destination is the city of Labyrinthos, where I plan to become an adventurer. As the name implies, Labyrinthos is home to a massive labyrinth that houses a swath of monsters. There, I'll be able to raise my fighting ability by accumulating actual combat experience in addition to completing quests as an adventurer, which means I'll also be helping people in need—two birds with one stone.

"Aria, are you really leaving?"

It's my mother. She's shaking with worry on the morning of my departure and has her marine-blue eyes locked on me. She's a bit overprotective. Maybe it's because of that kidnapping incident or that time I was nearly killed by demons—but she's always stuck to my side.

"It's going to be all right, Mother dear. I'm quite capable of using these knives, and I've been blessed with an innate skill. I will be a full-fledged warrior by the time I return."

"*Sigh…* Well, it looks like you've made up your mind. You better take care of yourself out there, okay?! And don't forget to come back to visit once in a while."

Seeing how firm my resolve is, my mother says her farewells and hugs me with all her strength.

"Whoa, look at that!"

"Yeah, Leona's and Aria's double melons are a sight!"

Hugging outside the front door was...a mistake. Two men walking along the road see us embracing and squawk in excitement. My mom's chest is about as big as mine, and she's about the same height. In other words, whenever we share a hug, our breasts press right up against each other.

The atmosphere is ruined. My mother sighs deeply and stifles a bitter laugh as she says, "Off you go, now" to send me on my way.

"Heh-heh, she's a real looker, isn't she?!"

"Yeah, and check out that rack! Will you *partner up* with me?"

How unbelievably atrocious.

A few days after reaching Labyrinthos and arranging the inn where I'll stay, I drop by the guild to register as an adventurer.

Just as I turn to approach the reception desk, I get accosted by two men. One of them is short and muscular, looking like a stubby, squat doll. The other one is tall, but he's gaunt and cloaked in a robe.

Judging from their appearance, there's no doubt these two are a swordsman and a mage, respectively. Tags that serve as proof these two are adventurers hang from their necks.

They're bronze in color, meaning they're D-ranked adventurers, if I recall correctly. This color denotes a full-fledged adventurer.

It's only midafternoon, but they're both red in the face, and their collective breath reeks of alcohol. Judging by their words and the way they're shamelessly leering up and down at my chest and legs, *partnering up* can mean only one thing.

"Excuse me. I have no interest in..."

This might be a pair of drunks, but they're also my seniors as adventurers. I have a long future ahead of me, so I try to deflect with what I intend to be a harmless diversion and head for reception. But...

"Just a minute now, young lass."

The squat, muscular man forcefully grabs my arm.

*Shudder...*

Fear courses through my entire body. As you know, I am extremely averse to human males due to past experiences. When the fear finally recedes, I can hear a cry echoing throughout the guild.

"Agyahhhh—!!"

"You bitch! What the hell did you do to my partner?!"

A man with eyes bulging out of his head furiously screams at me. Next to him, the muscular little fellow is holding his crotch and writhing in agony.

That's right. I was so appalled at being touched by the short one that I kicked him in the ba—*ahem*—in his weak point.

"......"

The scene seems to awaken something inside me. A brawny man writhing on the ground in pain, simply from being kicked in the crotch by my scrawny leg. The thought of that...feels invigorating. (Just a little bit, you know?)

*I wonder what would happen if I really kicked him?*

I can't help but idly wonder about it.

"You're dead meat!!"

The muscular one screams. His anger reaching a breaking point, he ignores the pain in his crotch to launch himself at me. His hand is on the hilt of his sword—this man must be serious.

I have only a slim chance of coming out on top against a D-ranked adventurer. But if I'm only looking to run away, I have my innate skill, Acceleration.

As he draws his sword, I activate my skill and start to distance myself...or at least I try...

"Wha—?!"

The muscular man cries out again and is stopped dead in his tracks. The blood drains from his face, and he's shaking like a leaf as he stares at me...or rather, behind me.

"Oh my. Did I just see you even thinking about drawing your weapon inside the guild? And are the two of you ganging up on a girl? Do you want to find out what it feels like to be a couple of feet underground? Huh??!!"

""Oh shiiiiiiiiiiiiit!!""

A man has appeared behind me... No, it's a woman, I think, with the huskiest voice that seems to rumble from deep within the earth as she intimidates the two men.

The pair looks pitiful as they yelp and scramble back to whatever hole they came from. I suppose it's only natural—the person standing behind me is...over six feet tall, completely clean-shaven, and absolutely ripped, sporting a full bondage gimp suit that covers her (his) muscles...

"Are you okay there, elf girl?"

"Y-yes! Thank you so much for saving me...ummm..."

"Oh, so sorry for not introducing myself earlier. My name is Arnold Holzweilzenegger, and I'm the receptionist at this guild. Call me Anna, okay?"

"My name is Aria. I came here to become an adventurer. It's very nice to meet you, Anna!"

I reply to Arnold Holzweilzenegger—Anna—as enthusiastically as I can. Anna is a bit...no, absolutely a curious sight to behold, but the fact of the matter is she saved me, and I can tell she is a very soft and gentle maiden from the sweet look in her eyes.

Elves have sharp instincts. We can generally determine if someone is an evildoer or not with a single glance. And in this case, my instincts seem to be dead-on. Since I mentioned that I'd like to become an adventurer, Anna explains the ABC's of adventuring to me with great care.

From that point on, every time I return from a quest, she checks to make sure I'm not injured or harmed in any way. She's just like a really caring older sister.

Because I'm a beginner, the first quests I take on mostly involve gathering items and defeating lower-level monsters—slimes and goblins.

To be honest, it's depressing to fight disgusting goblins every single day. But as long as I remind myself that this is training to become a warrior like the Sword Saint, it's easy to put up with.

Treating every quest seriously is very rewarding, and after carrying on like that for a while, I advance from the introductory level of E rank and become a D-ranked adventurer.

The very next day, I make a fateful acquaintance…

"Okay, another day, another chance to do my best!"

Even though I've reached D rank, I still haven't been able to form a party, which means trying anything risky is still forbidden. Today, I'm going back into the labyrinth to defeat more goblins on the first level.

"Is that a…kitty? What's it doing in the labyrinth…?"

After spending some time searching for goblins, I spot a tiny kitty that's just barely visible. Under normal conditions, there's no way an animal would wander into the labyrinth. I'm a bit suspicious of what might be going on here.

Further, the kitty is lying on its side and isn't moving. Maybe it's taking a nap, or maybe…

I get worried and decide to move closer. I absolutely adore kitties—I could never ignore one that got lost down here in the labyrinth.

"…!! Oh my, he's in trouble…!"

My eyes grow wide—the kitty has a huge gash on his torso. He must have gotten separated from his mother and been attacked by a monster while he was down here.

"He's still breathing. Don't worry—I'll heal you…!"

I withdraw a healing potion from the utility belt around my thigh and administer it to the kitty. Potions have an immediate curative effect. They can't remedy disability or dismemberment, but they will heal any general wound.

Normally, you're supposed to drink the potion, but they still work to some extent when applied directly to the wound. The kitty was unconscious, so I couldn't have him drink it anyway.

"Okay, your wound has closed up, and your breathing is more even, but your body's still cold…"

The only thing I can do now is warm up the kitty and pray that his will to live can save him. Holding the kitty, I rush back to my room at the inn. The innkeeper is a kind woman. When I tell her what's happened, she says she'll let me care for the little guy in my room.

That night—

*Rustle.*

The kitty wakes up and slowly rises on my bed. He's studying the room with a puzzled look. I'm so glad. It seems like he's going to be okay.

I can't help myself and give the kitty a big hug. Apparently, that surprised him, because he keeps blinking, but staying like that for a bit must have helped him relax—he's drifting off in my arms.

*He is the cutest little thing!*

Looking at the kitty, now comfortably curled up on my chest, I can't help but think how adorable he is.

He has orange tabby fur, and his sleepy eyes are a clear golden color. He's so tiny, he could completely hide in my two hands, and he has the most charming little face of any cat I've ever seen…

My pri—*ahem*—my chest starts throbbing uncontrollably.

Setting that aside—a few hours later, it's the start of a new day, and what a wonderful day it is. Sleeping while hugging this absolutely lovely ball of fur all night was already amazing—but this morning, he nuzzled into my chest with his little head, cuddling with me.

I wonder if he's mistaken me for his mama? In that case, he'll want milk…but I don't have any to offer him.

Wow…nipple play—with a kitty…!! But this isn't the time to think about that. I want to spoil this cat with my whole heart, but I have something to take care of first… Today is the cutoff for finishing my quest to hunt down goblins.

The thought of being apart is painful, but I put the kitty down on my bed and begin changing clothes. As I start to take off the negligee I sleep in…

*Mmmnnn…*

I feel a bit excited because the kitty is staring intensely at me as I change.

I mean, if such an adorable kitty saw you in your underwear, you would feel the same…right?

My privates start to feel a little tingly…

My panties…are fine. I won't need to change them.

Okay, all done changing. Time to set off on my adventure!

A short while later, I end up making a huge mistake on my quest, but kitty appears to save me just in the nick of time!

That's when I realize—this is no ordinary kitty. And I fall in love with him—the kitty that saves my life—Tama. But that's a story for next time…

# 🐾 Afterword 🐾

Thank you for purchasing this volume, and a special thanks to those who have been following the web versions. This is the author, Nozomi Ginyoku.

What exactly should an afterword entail...? I'm not entirely sure myself, so please allow me to start things off by explaining how this novel came to be published.

As mentioned above, this novel was originally posted on the online novel site known as Shousetsuka ni Narou before eventually getting revised into the volume you hold in your hands now.

I am thankful for the great reception it received from that initial serialization and how it rose to number one on the site's daily rankings only a few days after I published the first part.

After a few more days, a number of publishers approached me to feel out the possibility of turning this story into a published novel.

Reaching number one on the rankings was already like a dream come true for me, so having a real book published was...unbelievable. My heart raced with every new message I received on the site. Out of all of them, I felt a real connection with Micro Magazine.

The only reason I've come this far is all thanks to Micro Magazine, the incredible illustrations created by Mitsuki Yano, and of course, all my readers who have followed along since the web version.

Thank you all from the bottom of my heart. Please accept my gratitude and also this small plug (lol).

Some of you may already know, but this series is now also being serialized as a manga. The publisher is Hakusensha, and it's being published in the magazine *Young Animal Arashi*. The manga artist is Taro Shinonome.

Seeing the way Tama and Aria come to life in the illustrations, mewing and bouncing around together, is a must! Please take a look if you have a chance, and when the manga volume is released, please buy one! Call that direct marketing!

I believe that's all I have to say. I hope this volume sells well, and I look forward to seeing you all again in Volume 2!

## VERY STYLIZED

### Big eyes

### Small eyes

## SLIGHTLY LARGER PROPORTIONS

# Early Sketches of Aria and Vulcan by Mitsuki Yano

Aria

Vulcan